S0-BMZ-339

The Lost Sheep

THE MACMILLAN COMPANY
NEW YORK · CHICAGO
DALLAS · ATLANTA · SAN FRANCISCO
LONDON · MANILA

THE MACMILLAN COMPANY
OF CANADA, LIMITED
TORONTO

The Lost Sheep

by

HENRY BORDEAUX
of the French Academy

Translated by
FRANCES FRENAYE

Theodore Lownik Library
Illinois Benedictine College
Lisle, Illinois 60532

New York
THE MACMILLAN COMPANY
1955

843.9
B7276E

COPYRIGHT © 1955 BY
THE MACMILLAN COMPANY

All rights reserved—no part of this book may be repro-
duced in any form without permission in writing from
the publisher, except by a reviewer who wishes to quote
brief passages in connection with a review written for
inclusion in magazine or newspaper.

FIRST PRINTING

Printed in the United States of America

This book was published in the French
language under the title *La Brebis
Égarée*, copyright, 1953, by Librairie Plon.

47589

*To the memory
of the poet Francis Jammes,
author of the play The Lost Sheep,
I dedicate this novel
of the same title.*

H. B.

Contents

The Lost Sheep

I

The Stranger

"THE monks are back! The monks are back!"
At Saint-Pierre-de-Chartreuse, at Saint-Pierre-d'Entremont, which is separated from it only by the Cucheron Pass, at Saint-Laurent-du-Pont, across Le Désert, all the way to Le Sappey, La Ruchère and the near-by chalets of Bovinant, this rumor spread almost as rapidly as that of the Armistice, and to some degree counterbalanced it. The monastery was open again, even if half destroyed, and the village was saved although three-quarters under occupation. Mothers waited for the return of their soldier sons, no longer in danger, and the monastery was besieged by a crowd of vagabonds, beggars, and good people mindful, from generation to generation, of eight hundred years of prayers and good works who now came with offerings to their benefactors.

"Have you a place to lodge me?"

"Charity, in God's name."

"I've brought some fresh eggs . . ."

"You have no potatoes? I'll bring you a sack. Only it's a heavy load to carry up the hill."

1

"Here; take this. You'll say a mass or two for my beloved dead . . ."

On June 21, 1940, after thirty-seven years of enforced absence brought about by the laws against religious orders, the Carthusians had come back to the Grande Chartreuse Monastery, founded by Saint Bruno in 1084.

But the Prior had with him only two monks, the Bursar and Dom Béranger, who in this story of 1940 plays the part of a confessor and also a disciplinarian and mover of souls, and two lay brothers, one of them the gatekeeper and the other in charge of cooking and cleaning. The condition of the monastery was so lamentable that the members of the Order, who had been living in exile across the border, were not yet able to return. Nevertheless, appearances were kept up, on account of visitors, and the full extent of the destruction was visible only upon gradual penetration of the monastery. No more than three or four cells remained intact, and these were the ones shown to the public. The others had crumbled, from top to bottom. In spite of the ruin and decay, the sight of the Grande Chartreuse, bathed by the late June sun, made the Prior rejoice. The Prior was charged with the task of reconstruction, and in order to lighten his burden he had delegated the procurement of supplies to the Bursar, Dom Bernard, and all dealings with outsiders, including beggars, to Dom Béranger.

The Lost Sheep

Among the French fathers who had left the Italian monastery of Farneta for a temporary domicile at Voiron, Dom Béranger had been a logical choice for this mission because he knew both the place and its inhabitants. His monastic name disguised the fact that he belonged to the nobility of Dauphiné, whose castles nestle at the foot of the Chartreuse range, along the Isère River, at La Terrasse, Le Touvet, and Tencin. He had originally been a neighbor of the Marquis d'Arnay, famous for his kennels and his goat hunts, whose only daughter, Sylvie d'Arnay, last of her line, had left her magnificent home to an orphan asylum. A few years after marrying for love at the age of thirty, he had been called up in 1914 for war duty as a reserve officer of the Chasseurs Alpins; and he won three or four citations and the cross of the Legion of Honor. Almost immediately after demobilization he lost his wife and little daughter in the influenza epidemic; and because poison gas had affected his liver he was sent to Bagni di Lucca, near Florence, whose mineral waters and favorable climate contributed to the cure of all sorts of diseases. In his case, nerves and heart, rather than war injuries, were in need of care. He had survived all the risks of battle only to lose his adored wife and the child of their love. In his despair he doubted the existence of God, quite understandably, since all of us are inclined to blame Divine Providence for our misfortunes. During this period he visited the near-by monastery of Farneta, refuge of the Carthusians expelled from France at the turn of the century. There he met a monk he had known as a chaplain at Verdun, with whom he had lost touch because they were attached to different corps; and he heard that this friend Dom Geoffroy had been killed at Fort Malmaison while bringing aid to a soldier too seriously wounded to be transported to the rear. Nevertheless, the serenity of the monks was calming to his spirit. Among them he found balm for his wound, resignation through prayer, peace of mind in renewed faith.

"What if I were to stay on here with you?" he asked the Prior, when the time for departure was at hand. "I've thought it all over. I shall be faithful to the memory of my wife, that I know, and never marry again. Let me go back and arrange to dispose of my estate. My house and lands adjoin the orphanage founded by Sylvie d'Arnay, and I can present them to it. I have an income sufficient for my needs, so that I shall not be a burden upon your community."

The Carthusian Prior smiled at this. He felt sure that wealth, social position and sheer habit would soon regain the upper hand with this postulant. Good health and the passage of time bring forgetfulness of the most tragic hours, and even of those happy ones so briefly possessed before they were taken away. How could any man go on living without being able to forget? But Béranger surprised him by coming back three months later.

"I've used this time to put my affairs in order," he said. "Now I belong to God and to you."

He still had to meet the test of the severe Carthusian rule: he who had been accustomed to command must serve as a simple lay brother. And, having given proof of his humility, he must study theology and prepare himself for the priesthood.

"Hunting and war are more in my line," was his smiling answer to the Prior's questioning.

The Prior was an obstinate man. He put the postulant through five or six years of theological studies before ordination and the celebration of his first mass, which came as the fulfillment of all his prayers.

In 1940 Dom Béranger had been a Carthusian for fifteen years, years which he had devoted to contemplation and meditation that blended thoughts of death with life divine. He was sixty, tall, erect, and gray-bearded. It gave him joy to return to the austere Chartreuse scene where in his youth he had so often hunted goats, wood grouse, and white partridge. The Prior was amazed to find that he remembered every road and path.

"And yet no one has recognized me in my habit," Dom Béranger told him. "I've changed too much in twenty-five years."

The monastic rule had not yet been fully reestablished, and the fathers ate with the lay brothers: meals sometimes meager, sometimes enriched by the generosity of the faithful who were deeply moved by their return. One July evening at eight o'clock, when their frugal supper was drawing to a close, there was a ring of the bell, at first so timid that the gatekeeper, rounding off his soup with a piece of cheese, paid no attention. The ringing became insistent, and finally the Prior said:

"It's unlikely that anyone should intrude upon us at this late hour. But you'd better go see."

A big, blonde peasant woman with a red scarf around her head and a black shawl over her shoulders asked desperately to see one of the Carthusians.

"The Prior? He can't be disturbed at this hour."

"Whoever's in charge—that's the one I want to see."

"Do you know him personally?"

"How should I know him, when he's just arrived?"

"And what do you want?"

"That's my own affair."

"Come back tomorrow."

"No, I want to hand over my burden tonight."

In her arms she had a tiny lamb, so black that it could scarcely be distinguished from her shawl.

"Take it," she said to the brother.

He went back to the refectory with the lamb.

"There's a woman at the door who won't go away."

"Ask her what she wants."

"She won't tell me."

"Then you must go, Dom Béranger. Find out what has brought her here at this hour, and thank her for the lamb."

"Is she young or old?" Dom Béranger asked.

"I didn't notice," the lay brother answered. "Judging from the way she walked, I should say she might be young."

Dom Béranger acting on the Prior's advice, arranged to receive this unusual visit in the cemetery instead of his half-ruined cell.

The sun was still playing over the gravestones and the wild flowers among them when the lay brother brought the peasant woman there. She was still young, perhaps thirty, and walked with the swaying gait of a barefoot gypsy. As she drew close to his white habit she knelt on the ground.

"Forgive me," she said humbly.

Somewhat taken aback, Dom Béranger asked if she had come to make a confession, and when she said no, he raised her to her feet.

"You're unhappy," he said. "Are you married?"

"Yes, sir—yes, Father."

Apparently she was not used to members of a religious order and did not know how to address him.

"Have you children?"

"Yes, Father—two. A girl and a boy."

"Are they well?"

"I don't know."

7

He looked at her intently and saw that she was beautiful and disconsolate. But her eyes did not meet his.

"Is there peace within you and within your home?"

Suddenly she made up her mind to speak out.

"That's why I'm here. You have come home. Please make it possible for me to go home too. As soon as I heard that you had returned I wanted to do the same thing."

The comparison was so unexpected that the monk smiled.

"Were you sent away, like us?"

"Yes, Father."

"We've been away thirty-seven years. And you?"

"Five years, Father."

"We were put out by the Combes government. Who put you out?"

"My husband."

"We monks passed our exile in fasting and prayer. Can you say as much?"

She was silent.

"Why did your husband send you away?"

"Because of—Séverin."

"And who is Séverin?"

"A shepherd. One of those Provence shepherds who bring their sheep to graze in the mountains every summer. They lodge in the chalets at Bovinant, close to the top of the pass and the beginning of the descent to Saint-Pierre-d'Entremont."

"Yes, I know the place. Was it he that seduced you?"

"Oh, I was just as much to blame as he. I'm quite aware of my guilt. But on their account I've suffered so dreadfully—"

"On account of your children?"

"Yes, Father. Lise was six years old, and Pierre three. Now they're eleven and eight. They've grown up without me."

"What about your husband?"

"He is a good man, really, but on this occasion he was very hard. He had a right to beat me, but he shouldn't have sent me away. The children were too small. A wife can always be replaced, but not a mother."

"And why were you unfaithful to him?"

"Who knows? We lived at La Ruchère, and I had gone to Bovinant to buy a pregnant ewe. The baby lambs were to be for the children. Séverin was the first one I met. He played the flute and the accordion. When he laughed he had a whole row of white teeth. He told all sorts of entertaining stories, and he could see that I was smiling at them. He tried to kiss me, and I slapped him across the face."

"That was the right thing to do."

"But he wasn't so easily discouraged. He came

to La Ruchère, again and again. Everyone enjoyed his music. But he came there to see me."

Dom Béranger listened as patiently as Jesus had listened to the woman taken in adultery.

"Did your husband catch you?"

"Yes, he was told by a neighbor. They gossip in the villages. Life is all hard work and ill will. They can't tolerate other people's love, even when it's legal. And so my husband was alerted. One day he saw Séverin with his arm around me. I had a feeling he was there, and I ran away and got home before him. I kept the children close to me while I lit the fire in the kitchen stove. That way, I thought he wouldn't raise a hand against me. Because I had every reason to expect a beating. But he didn't beat me at all. He didn't say a word; he simply pointed to the door. I didn't understand, or rather I didn't want to, until finally I couldn't help it. He marched straight at me and threw me out. I'll always hear my daughter's cry. For a day or two I simply wandered about. Finally I was hungry and went to Bovinant. Séverin took me in. He thought it wouldn't last, but it went on for five years."

"And now what has happened?"

"He kept me with him all summer. Then, at the end of September, came the time for him to take his flock back to the plains. He lived near Arles with his father and mother, and on their account he didn't want to take me along. He did take me, though, and told them that we were married. They looked at me suspiciously, but they accepted me as one of the family. The plains are warm and sunny. There's outdoor bowling and other games. It's an easy-going country, a place for good times rather than hard work. Still there are poor people who manage to make a living. I'm an early riser and a hard worker myself, and I found all sorts of heavy jobs to do. But Séverin didn't like it. Because he had passed me off as his wife he wanted me all to himself, to wait upon him. And so that's how I've lived these last five years: the winter in Provence and the summer up at Bovinant. Each summer when we arrived in the mountains, with our sheep and donkeys, I was always frantic with wanting to see them . . ."

"To see whom?"

"Lise and Pierrot, my children. I used to go all the way up to the pass and over to La Ruchère. There I hid, so that no one would report me."

"And who would have done a thing like that?"

"The neighbors. They'd have called my husband. I kept watch until he left the house, and then I went closer. Surely a mother has a right to look at her children, without their knowing. After I had seen them, I ran away."

"And what have you done with Séverin now?"

"He didn't come up this summer, Father. He was taken into the army, but they released him so that he could attend to his animals. In May he said to me: 'You go ahead to Bovinant and open the chalet. I'll come after you, with the sheep.' I got there first, as we

had planned, and the sheep came after, but with another shepherd, an old man. 'Where's Séverin?' I asked
him. But he only made fun of me. 'Séverin? He's got
himself married, to a girl in Arles.' 'And what about
me?' 'You? Well, all he said to me was: "She'll make
out all right. Women can always manage, somehow." '
At first I wouldn't believe it. But then I had to admit
that it was true. Séverin had deserted me. I went back
to La Ruchère, but I didn't dare try to see my husband.
I have no place to live. The old man expected to take
Séverin's place with me, but I'm not that kind. I left
my own ewe behind and took a lamb, the one I brought
here this evening. . . . Father, you must save me.
You must make it possible for me to go home."

"Exactly what do you want me to do?"

"To go to La Ruchère and ask for my man.
Joachim Corbier is his name. Our house is above the
church, at Reverdy, beside the tavern."

"And what shall I say to him?"

"You'll find the right thing to say. He's a hard man
but a good Christian. A visit from one of the monks
that have just come back will surely touch his heart.
You can tell him that I've suffered and am sorry. If
he'll let me into the house, he'll never know that I'm
there, except for the cooking and cleaning. But I must
have my children."

"I don't think he'll accept that kind of bargain."

"Then let him take me back altogether. My only
hope is in you. I've been thinking of the river."

Dom Béranger read the suicidal intention in her dry eyes.

"You mustn't look at the river. You must raise your eyes to heaven and pray. I'll go tomorrow to La Ruchère. You can wait for me in the church. May God protect you and help me to perform my task!"

"In the church, then. Oh, yes, I'll be waiting!"

"Meanwhile, where are you going to pass the night?"

"There's a stable."

"Have you a blanket?"

"I've no need of that. Goodbye, Father, until tomorrow. I have faith in you."

And with the same swinging gait she went confidently away.

II

La Ruchère

AFTER the woman had gone, Dom Béranger realized that he had spoken too quickly in promising to meet her at the church of La Ruchère. Even though the Carthusian rule had not yet been re-established, he must ask the Prior's permission to absent himself the whole day on an errand of this kind. In a few words he explained the woman's situation.

"She wants to follow our example and go home. I don't know how successful I shall be in winning over her husband, whom she describes as a good Christian but a hard man. Can one be pitiless and a good Christian?"

The Prior answered by leafing through his missal to the gospel for the third Sunday after Pentecost and presenting the open book to the other:

What man of you that hath an hundred sheep, and if he shall lose one of them, doth he not leave the ninety-nine in the desert, and go after that which was lost, until he find it? and when he hath found it, lay it upon his shoulders, rejoicing, and coming home, call together his friends and neighbors, saying to them: "Rejoice with me, because I have found my sheep that was lost"?

And he added:

"This woman has given us a lamb. But she herself is a lost sheep, and you must lead her back home."

"I don't know whether I shall be able to do it."

"Stop and say a prayer to Notre-Dame de Casalibus."

"Yes, that shrine is on my way."

"So you already know the road to La Ruchère?"

"Two hours to the top of the pass, and then one hour down to the village," said Dom Béranger with a smile. "I've been going there for the last seven hundred years."

"Seven hundred years?"

"Yes, I've counted them carefully. When I was putting my affairs in order before taking my vows, I came across a deed of gift drawn up in the middle of the twelfth century by my ancestor Aymon de Corbel, Squire of Les Echelles. For the salvation of his soul and and that of Florence, his wife, he gave to the Grande Chartreuse his property at La Ruchère and the services of the peasants living upon it."

"Then you have rights over this parish!"

"The donation didn't actually take place without some difficulty. The Bishop of Grenoble, a former Carthusian named Jean de Sassenage, managed to put the transfer through during a short stay at the monastery, since the donor didn't seem to be in any hurry. The Prior sent Brother Eynard to remind the Squire of his promise. Aymon de Corbel was warned of his coming and went into hiding in the mountains. Brother Eynard took a notary along, and the two overtook the Squire in a stable. The notary called for a table and drew up, right there, a deed by virtue of which the Squire robbed himself and his heirs to the extent of turning the property over to Brother Eynard as representative of the Carthusians. That is the story, exactly as I found it in my family papers."

"Then good luck to you on your errand," said the Prior. "May you be just as successful as Brother Eynard, seven hundred years ago!"

III

The Meeting

IT is, indeed, a trip of at least two or three hours
from the monastery to La Ruchère: a stiff climb
to the pass and then an endless descent through the
woods on the other side. The sun rises early in July,
and Dom Béranger started before the sun, stopping
on the way at the chapel of Notre-Dame de Casalibus,
or Our Lady of the Cabins. The original chapel had
been erected in the desert by St. Hugh; in the twelfth
century an avalanche swept it away, and after suc-
cessive rebuilding and restoration, it rises now like a
flower amid the pines whose roots are entwined about
its stones. Near by is another chapel, dedicated to St.
Bruno, founder of the Carthusians, on the site of a
fountain where he used to come for refreshment. Dom
Béranger prayed to these two patron saints in behalf
of the woman who was seeking pardon without a true
sense of remorse, and longing for the children whom
she had lost through no one's fault but her own.

The crisp mountain air caressed his face, and the
green trees sheltered him from the sun, which was
rising now above the mountains. He walked through
fields, bordered by a stream, where cattle were graz-

ing, until he came to the pass. Here he could not help stopping to look at the view ahead and behind. Ahead lay the pale blue Lake Bourget, with its outlines softened by the light mist which in good weather frequently hangs over it and the surrounding slopes. Beyond the lake was the chain of the Bauges mountains, in which the Grand-Columbier and the Arcalod stood out. Closer was the rugged Granier, and directly below, in the shadow, the Frou valley, with the Guiers-Vif River, whose rushing sound echoed all the way up to where he stood. Behind him were the heights of the Chartreuse: the Grand-Som with rocks white as snow, and Chamechaude, like a miniature Matterhorn with an army of pines and cedars growing up its sides. Dom Béranger looked at all these wonders and smiled and prayed, offering to God the joy he found in His creation.

How could he feel so happy, when the loss of his adored wife and daughter had taken from him his hopes for the future and condemned him to a life of solitude, when he who had contributed to his country's victory in the Great War now saw it two-thirds occupied by the Germans? Just then an incident in his youth came to mind. In the course of his convalescence from one of the rare attacks of some childhood disease —measles or scarlet fever—that interrupted his general good health, his mother had read aloud to him an autobiographical novel, A Nun's Story, which had charmed her own younger years but seemed to him slightly ridiculous in the extravagance of its piety and in the purity of its passion. The heroine, Alexandrine d'Alopeus, happily married to Albert de la Ferronnays, turned to God after the early death of her husband. Later, as she was losing the bloom of youth, a friend was amazed by her serenity and asked: "If you were to recover Albert, wouldn't you be happy?" She answered: "I'd not dream of raising him from the dead." So now Dom Béranger knew that he would not dream of raising his wife and daughter. By their death they had given him that confidence in God, that abandonment which makes for death-in-life, that is, for continual awareness of the divine presence and the constant thought of immortality which he shared with the other monks, his companions in the execution of God's will. And so he had reason to be happy, and he gave thanks to his Creator for the beautiful scene around him. Even the misfortunes of his martyred country were powerless to shake his faith in a help from God which is the answer to prayer.

He walked hopefully down toward the little church with the wide transept and the spire that was pointed like a lance at the sky. A short cut took him through the woods which border the pastures of Aliénard, above the left bank of the Guiers-Vif and then he rejoined the road to Les Chartreux and Les Mouilles, two hamlets composed almost entirely of barns, Le Grand Village and Reverdy. The church was a short distance beyond. As Dom Béranger knelt there, asking God's aid in his undertaking, a woman who had entered before him came over and said in a low voice, as if begging for charity:

"Father, I'm here."

Raising his head, Dom Béranger recognized the face he had seen the day before. She had wound a scarf around her head before entering the sacred place.

"I have not yet seen your husband," he protested.

"I'm afraid, Father."

"You'll have to wait."

"But I'd like to make my confession."

She was sorry, then, for her sin. She was ending where she should have begun. The prayers he had addressed to Hugh and Bruno were already bearing fruit, for she had come herself to make reparation; and his morning was not lost, since her soul was saved. He took her over to the confessional, listened while she wept, and finally granted her absolution.

"Wait for me here," he said. "I'll come back for you."

"But I know he won't have me, Father."

"How can you know?"

"Tell him I'll be content to return as his servant."

Joachim Corbier's house was in Reverdy, through which he had just passed, near the tavern. Dom Béranger knocked at the door, but there was no answer. A neighbor saw his white habit. Was it possible? Dear God! She had heard that the monks were back— and here was one of them! Like St. Thomas with

Christ's wounds, she wanted to touch his habit. She wanted to run and spread the good news. But the father stopped her, with a finger at his lips. He was requiring of her the hardest thing of all: silence. Very well, then, she would be silent.

"You can go right in, Father," she told him. "Joachim Corbier should be back any minute. He hasn't yet eaten his morning soup. And the children must be there. I take care of them."

She did not know that he had come on a mission of peace, to reconcile husband and wife. Otherwise, she would have been suspicious, for she was on almost too intimate terms with her neighbor. While she went to fetch Joachim, the monk entered. In the kitchen, which served as a dining room as well, he found the little girl filling her brother's plate. Neither was afraid of this man in white, who smiled and called them by name.

"You're Lise, and you're Pierrot."

"Yes, sir."

"And where's your father?"

"He'll be coming soon."

"And your mother?"

No reply.

"You do have a mother, don't you?"

"I don't know," said the girl doubtfully.

"I haven't any," said the little boy, "or rather I have several. They're always changing."

"Be quiet," said the girl, who was more knowing.

"Doesn't your father ever speak of her?"

The Lost Sheep

"No," said Lise, turning suddenly sad.

How much did she know? Little girls are so quick to understand! But Joachim Corbier was coming in.

"You have two handsome children, Joachim Corbier. But they need a mother. Look at the holes in their clothes and the dirt on their sweet faces!"

Joachim was amazed at his quick comprehension. How had he guessed that the wife was away? He wasn't a magician.

"She's dead," said Joachim. Was it to get rid of the monk or simply to put him to trial?

"My friend, you know very well that's not true. But send these children to your neighbor, who's waiting for them."

Why should he send the children away? Joachim was mistrustful. The white-robed monk knew entirely too much. Nevertheless, he obeyed. Hand in hand, Lise and Pierrot went out the door.

"Yes," said Dom Béranger, "you've guessed it. Joachim Corbier, I've come on behalf of the wife you sent away five years ago."

"I only did what was right."

"No, my friend, that's not true. You listened to the voice of anger, jealousy, and pride. You thought only of yourself, and not of your unfortunate wife and children."

Joachim had never looked at the matter from this point of view, never considered the full implications of marriage. He had been sure he was within his rights, and now those rights were called into question. He respected the vocation of priest, and even more a monk returned from exile to the mountain monastery. But the words he had just heard stirred feelings which had been covered up by the years, and opened a wound which he had thought was closed forever.

"What she did is quite unforgivable, Father."

"God goes right on forgiving us, my son."

"That's different. He's God, and you're clergy. Besides, for you, women don't exist."

"You're wrong, Joachim Corbier. Women are God's creatures, and your wife exists so definitely for me that I am bringing her back to you."

"I don't want her."

"I'm not bringing back the adulterous wife whom you cast out of your house. I'm bringing you an unfortunate woman who has obtained God's forgiveness and who humbly seeks yours."

"It's too old a story. She's too late. At first it hurt, but now I'm used to getting along without her." Then, contradicting his proclaimed indifference, he asked: "What's she done with that shepherd of hers?"

"He left her, to marry another woman."

"Ah, so that's it!"

Like a wandering sheep, she wanted to come back to the fold for food and shelter, and this priest was her accomplice. But he wouldn't fall in with her scheme. So she too had been deserted! So much the worse for her! Let her beg bread from strangers!

Dom Béranger read all these evil thoughts on the peasant's hard face.

"You're wrong again, Joachim Corbier. She's young enough and strong enough to earn her living. It's not on the shepherd's account that she came near to killing herself."

"Killing herself?"

"Yes, and it's not on his account, but on account of you and the children. She can't escape from the memory; it pursues her day and night. That's why she came to me and said: 'You have come home and are happy. Help me to go home, too.' I didn't really want to interfere, but I saw death in her eyes. You wouldn't want to be responsible for her suicide, would you?"

"I never raised a hand against her."

"You did something much worse than that. You were pitiless at a time when you might have saved her. She was weak rather than bad. And now she is much stronger."

"I don't understand."

"Since this morning she has been strong. She has repented of her sin. Now she's a different woman. Joachim, do not send her away a second time. Later you'd be sorry. Your children would reproach you for taking part of their childhood away, for making orphans of them."

Contradictory impulses tugged at Joachim's heart.

"I don't want to do it. I can't. You don't know what it is to suffer."

"I know about all there is to know, Joachim. I

lost my wife and daughter, and went into holy orders
so that I might endure the loss and offer it to God. . . .
Let your wife come in through this same door from
which you ejected her. She's even willing to return as
a servant."

"A servant?"

This was exactly what Joachim Corbier needed.
The woman next door was demanding more money
for the care of his children, and pursuing him with her
advances. The monk's words had shaken him deeply,
and his resistance was tottering like that of an uprooted
tree. Besides, here was a chance to serve his natural
avarice. This Mélanie could cook and wash and look
after the children. He wouldn't look at her, or let her
eat at the same table. She could sleep in one of the
barns outside. Yes, this was a good enough solution.

"Very well, as a servant," he repeated.

Dom Béranger felt that victory was half won. A
man can't relinquish his pride too quickly. Perhaps
Joachim would give in little by little when he was
faced with both the humble presence of Mélanie and
his children's appeal to his feelings. The main thing
was that she should be there, that she should get into
the house, even by the back door.

"That's quite clear, is it then, Joachim? You'll take
her as a servant."

"That's not what I said, Father."

"Yes, it is. And you can't go back on your word.
I'm going to fetch her."

"Not yet. Not so soon."

"Yes. You mustn't leave her in distress. She's right there. I'll go call her."

"Where is she?"

"In God's house, where she was welcome from the start. In the church, Joachim."

Joachim could resist no longer.

"Very good, Father. As soon as I have had my soup, which is already cold, I'll be off to the sawmill. She can come to the house and start looking after the housework and the children. But she's not to tell them who she is."

"You are hard, Joachim."

But Dom Béranger knew that the children would be less severe. Soon enough they would be fond of her. Meanwhile Joachim was speaking again:

"When I come back from the sawmill I shan't look at her. And she's not to say a word to me."

"You're very hard, Joachim," the monk repeated.

"That's the only way I know how to be."

"Well, that's settled. I'll bring her back."

He rose, and his white habit seemed to light up the room. Joachim vaguely understood that the visitor was no ordinary man but a man of God. He wanted to add something to what he had said, but could not find the words. The bargain was struck. But was it really a matter of striking a bargain? Dom Béranger was gone now, and the light had left the room. Joachim hastily downed his bowl of thick soup, which had grown cold with waiting. He did not wish to be present when his wife arrived.

At the church that poor woman was waiting on her knees for her emissary's return. He had left her a rosary, but she lingered over every bead, sighing for her children. What chance was there of obtaining Joachim's forgiveness? She thought back to the beginning of her marriage. He had had money, and she had had none. At first he had attempted to have her without benefit of matrimony; but when he found out that she was virtuous he gave in. He had showered her with gifts, in spite of the fact that he was a miser, and broken away from his habitual sternness so far as to smile with her. The years they had spent together were happy. Why, then, had she been unfaithful to him? Now that Séverin had revealed himself to be such a coward, she couldn't find the reason. Séverin was forgotten, and her abandoned marriage filled her mind.

Dom Béranger entered the church, his white habit casting its light. He had learned that the local priest was not yet back from the army, and the curé of Saint-Pierre-d'Entremont came every Sunday to celebrate mass. He was disappointed, because now he could not ask the priest to watch over Mélanie and exercise his influence to have the villagers treat her with consideration. As things were, he had to do his best to bolster her courage.

"Mélanie Corbier, go home. Your trials are not over. Joachim is taking you in as a servant. Only by patience and humility can you hope to regain your former station. Don't lose heart. Your day will come, I promise you. One day you and your husband will come to the monastery, and you will come together. Meanwhile, if you need me, don't hesitate to call. Goodbye, and God bless you."

"Oh, Father! . . ."

She sobbed as he raised his hand in blessing and went away.

There was a clamor outside the door. The neighbor whom Dom Béranger had cautioned to be silent had not been able to comply, and had gone from door to door announcing the return of the Carthusian. Now the whole village had gathered to welcome him.

While he spoke from the church steps to the assembled crowd Mélanie Corbier slipped out by a side door. No one was waiting for her in the house—neither husband nor children. For a moment she stood motionless; then she picked up a broom and swept the kitchen floor. Next she made the children's beds, in a more loving manner than they had ever been made. After that she looked over their clothes. Most things were still in the same places, and she was able to find them in spite of a certain disorder. What a lot of work there was for her to do! But, after all, she was a servant in the house.

IV

The Return

WHEN Dom Béranger had freed himself from the sympathetic commotion caused by the sight of his white Carthusian habit, he started up through the village of La Ruchère, which rises in a series of tiers beyond the church, in the direction of the pass by which he had come. He turned to look back at the landscape of mountains and valleys, with Lake Bourget below, which sun and shadow had etched upon Savoy—a beneficiary of God's particular favor ever since the world first emerged from the waters. But he could not recover his earlier sensation of hope and joy. The fate of Mélanie Corbier weighed heavily upon him. He had given her into her husband's care; but Joachim was a hard-hearted, avaricious man and had assumed no obligations other than those of a master to a servant. It was Dom Béranger's hope that the children would restore Mélanie to their father's good graces; but the neighbor who looked after them had spoken of Joachim in a familiar manner which had not upset him at the time, but which came back now to harass him. What if she were Joachim's mistress? In the monk's austere judgment she was anything but attractive. No, if Joachim had been bound to her, he would never have Mélanie in the house, even in the capacity of a servant. Surely Joachim would forget Séverin, the accordion-player from Arles, who was never coming to Bovinant again, and would forgive the mother of Lise and Pierrot. Time is a great healer, as the saying goes, and no peasant has sufficient leisure to brood over an old injury and seek a tardy revenge.

But no matter how he rationalized it, Dom Béranger could not dispel his worry. At the top of the pass he paused before continuing down to the Grande Chartreuse. In spite of his sixty years, he was not tired. His heart beat regularly. He remembered that he had hunted mountain goats in this same place thirty or forty years ago, and that the master of the hunt had bid him lie in ambush over there in a clearing at the edge of the downward slope. Soon a female and her kid, pursued by the hunters and isolated from their fellows, had sprung into view. With the prey at his mercy, he had shouldered his gun and fired. The kid fell but got up again, for his kind must be dead to surrender. As for the female, she pushed him into a space between two rocks through which he might escape, although it was too narrow for her to follow. Then, placing herself between him and the hunter, she wheeled about and fearlessly waited for the man to shoot. He fired too quickly and only wounded her foot, while she maintained her attitude of defiance. A second shot struck her shoulder, and she bled heavily but did not falter.

When the third shot finally brought her down, the kid had disappeared.

The whole hunt had impressed Dom Béranger as being a form of organized murder, and that was why he remembered it so clearly. There were females, then, who would die for their young! He had gone with the guard who picked up the goat's body to the refuge where his companions were waiting. But toward dusk, he returned to the scene of the massacre, hoping to find the survivor. And there, sure enough, was the kid sniffing at the entrails, which had been cut out and left on the ground. This was the young animal's first acquaintance with death; he uttered a succession of plaintive wails in the lengthening shadows, as if they could give him back the mother who had sacrificed her own life for her kid. The young man had not the heart to shoot him. The next day the hunters would rest, and the kid would have time to rejoin the fleeing herd.

Why should Dom Béranger link this memory to the fate of Mélanie Corbier? In spite of her sinful passion, she had never forgotten her children; and now, for their sake, she had promised to put up with her husband's avarice and hardheartedness. Having at last come home, she faced the necessity of expiation. If only it were not too bitter for her to bear! If only Séverin of Arles did not come back to the mountains with his sheep! Should he go to Bovinant and inquire about him? The sun was still high in the sky, and the

July days were long. He had brought along a loaf of bread and a hard-boiled egg. Yes, that was it: he would make a detour to Bovinant.

Dom Béranger smiled as he recalled the pattern of the paths. He followed the Wolf's Trail, which goes around the south side of the Petit-Som, and soon had a view of the green meadows at the foot of the Grand-Som, contrasting with the pine trees and the white rocks. These meadows afford pasture to hundreds of sheep driven there to graze far from the dry Midi. With a few questions he had no trouble finding Séverin's sheep and the old shepherd who had them in his charge—a man of easy speech and familiar manner.

"Where's the accordion-player?" Dom Béranger asked.

"Ah, he's quite happy to be exactly where he is. That—with all due respect, Father—is wallowing with his new wife, a girl from Arles with as shapely a figure as you could hope to see. He can't leave her for a minute."

"Is he married, then?"

"All legal and proper! A civil wedding and a church one on top of it! To tell you the truth, he had a woman up here at Bovinant, and he's handed her on to me. She's gone off in a huff for the time being, taking a lamb with her; but I'm expecting her back. You don't happen to have seen her, do you?"

"Yes, I have." Using the authoritative tone of voice proper to a former army officer, Dom Béranger put the fellow in his place for making light of Mélanie's misfortune. "She's gone back to her husband, whom she should never have left in the first place. God punish the man that mocks her repentance or interferes with her good resolution! Yes, woe upon Séverin if he dares to show his face, and upon you if you continue to bother her! You're not to go near La Ruchère. Do you hear me?"

There must indeed have been authority in his voice, for the priest-baiting old shepherd immediately lost his brash assurance.

"I had no idea of going after her, Father!" he said fawningly.

"Then you're a wise man. It wouldn't be good for your health. You'd be greeted with a pitchfork, and Séverin would fare even worse than you. I now bid you goodbye."

As the Carthusian started away, the shepherd ran after him.

"Are you back, all of you?" he asked.

"Yes, we're back in our monastery which was stolen from us."

"Then I'll bring you some cheese."

"Please don't bother."

"Won't you have a drink of water, Father? It's a hot day."

"No, I must be off down the mountain."

The fellow wished at all costs to win the monk's favor, but his awkward advances met with no success.

With the long strides of a born mountaineer, Dom Béranger rapidly widened the distance between them. The descent was more fatiguing than the climb, and when he came to Notre-Dame de Casalibus, he sat down on the trunk of a tree. Then he went into the chapel and prayed to the Virgin to bless Mélanie Corbier's return to her home. Mélanie was the name of the young girl to whom the Virgin appeared at La Salette. Plainly her mother had had this miraculous apparition in mind and had wished to entrust her child to one whose protection has never been invoked in vain. It was with a feeling of reassurance that Dom Béranger rang at the monastery gate. Still he was not altogether easy in his mind, for the hard face of Joachim Corbier continued to haunt him. Why was it linked with his memory of the mountain goat saving her kid's life with her own?

V

The Neighbor

LA RUCHÈRE, at an altitude of three thousand feet, is composed of a series of hamlets which run from the pass overhanging the Grande-Chartreuse monastery down to the restored church, the school, and the town hall, the two last-named built or rebuilt some hundred years ago. It is reached from below by a road tributary to the one cut through the rock between Saint-Pierre-d'Entremont and Les Echelles, above the deep Frou valley, where the Guiers-Vif River, rich in perch and mountain trout, tumbles over a stony bed. Although the village is hardly visible among the surrounding cedars and pines, it commands a panoramic view over the distant Lake Bourget, between the two mountains known as the Granier and Corbelet.

Here are none of the pastures where sheep come from the south to graze in the summer. And the land is too wooded for agriculture. The peasants raise potatoes and other vegetables for their own consumption, sometimes a little wheat and oats to provide bread for themselves and fodder for their livestock, which may be two or three cows, rarely a goat, and a few ducks and chickens. Most of them depend on the forests:

they fell and cut trees with axes and power saws, and carry the logs away on trucks and tractors. The women make gloves—a cottage industry stemming from Grenoble, which makes for a moderate prosperity evidenced by the immaculate cleanliness of their houses and the flowers at every window.

When, by Dom Béranger's intervention, Mélanie Corbier returned to her home, she found no one there: Joachim had gone to the sawmill at the lower end of the village, where he cut cedars and beeches and made pine boards. His sawmill had given him exemption from army service: it was requisitioned by the government for military purposes, and he was left in charge. The children were still at school, which would continue until Bastille Day. Mélanie swept the house, made the beds, mended clothes, and started to peel some potatoes. She lit the fire in order to prepare a meal, but found nothing to cook but some cabbages and a bit of ham. All of a sudden she paused, confused by the sound of loud steps on the stairs. The kitchen, which served also as dining room, was on the second floor where it was less exposed to dampness and snow. Lise and Pierrot, vociferously arguing, burst into the room, under the direction of Péronne Grenier, the neighbor who had pointed out the house to Dom Béranger. The boy, wild and self-willed, stopped short in front of the intruder.

"Who's this?" he asked, turning to his sister.

Lise took a step forward, as if she had instinctively

recognized the mother whom she had lost when she
was six years old. But instinct did not long hold the
upper hand, and she stopped in her tracks, wondering,
like her brother, about this stranger who seemed to be
so much at home in preparing the meal. This moment
of uncertainty allowed Péronne Grenier, who had
dropped behind on the stairs, to overtake her charges
and come face to face with Mélanie. She was unmar-
ried, perhaps forty years old, heavily and powerfully
built, with a hatchet face reddened by exercise and
fresh air. At once she recognized Joachim Corbier's
banished wife; but unlike Dom Béranger, who had
looked into her soul, she made the approach of a horse
dealer who looks over a handsome mare and angrily
declares that the price the owner asks is much too high.
First of all, she was dismayed by Mélanie's youth—she
did not seem to be an hour older than when she had
gone away five years before—by her frank, open face
and naturally curly blond hair, now piled on top of
her head in disarray. Her own awkward attempts to
win the heart of Joachim were destined for failure
unless she could chase this intruder away. And so
she came forward and said scornfully:

"You here? Get out! Get out quickly!"

Face to face with Lise and Pierrot, Mélanie had
just gone through the fears and transports of mother-
love. She had not raised her arms, but held them
resolutely at her sides; she had not spoken the words
that surged to her lips, but tears had welled up in her

eyes. And it seemed as if Lise had somehow guessed at her feelings. Why did Péronne have to spoil this first moment, which was making up for so many years of separation? Well, some reply had to be made.

"I've been authorized—"

"Who authorized you? Get out of here! If Joachim should come!"

"He's the one who authorized—"

"Five years ago he put you out of this door for your sins. Well, it's too late now; I hear him coming. No doubt he'll get after you with a stick this time."

A man's step was heard on the stair. Pierrot was absorbed in what was going to happen next. He imagined the stranger running down the stair in order to escape a beating. But Lise at once took Mélanie's side and rushed to meet her father at the door.

"Oh, Father!"

Joachim knew well enough how matters stood, but Péronne had not been forewarned. Pointing to the newcomer, she shouted:

"Look, Joachim, there's your wife!"

The little girl caught the word "wife" immediately, and smiled as if to say: "I knew it all along." Of course she knew nothing; she only suspected, hoped, and vaguely understood that some day she would regain her mother.

Joachim gave his wife a single look, which seared and crushed her. She only wished she could melt into the ground, out of sight of her children. She remembered all too vividly the day when he had pointed to the door, when he had demanded that she go away and never again show herself before him. Seeing that he had forgotten nothing, she prepared to take leave. But to her surprise he answered the officious neighbor:

"Well, what of it?"

"How does she dare show her face here?"

"She's my new servant."

Péronne couldn't believe her ears. She laughed nervously, striving to hide her anger.

"Your servant? How much will you pay her?"

"Nothing."

"Ah, so you're saving money. And what about me?"

"I shan't need you any more."

"Don't I get a week's notice?"

"No."

In her anger she picked up a chair and broke it. Then she went out, slamming the door and tossing over her shoulder:

"You'll be hearing from me!"

Joachim was not proud of the way he had behaved. He had yielded to a bitterness directed equally at both women. All things considered, he could say nothing but good of his neighbor. She had taken pity on children who had been virtually abandoned and a man who was quite helpless around the house. The care of an old mother, crippled by rheumatism, kept her at home, but she did piecework for a Grenoble glovemaker and found time to wash and dress the little boy (the girl managed, although somewhat awkwardly, to take care of herself), sweep the house, and prepare dinner. Grateful for her services, he had agreed to make a modest payment for them. Eventually her mother had died, and in the last year she had seen more of him than before, occasionally eating dinner with him and staying part of the evening. Gradually he had become aware that she was pursuing him. After all, why not? He had had quite enough of enforced chastity, and although this woman's face did not particularly appeal to him, she had a solid, rounded figure of the kind much esteemed in the country. Nevertheless, he hadn't given in to her—at least not yet. Her advances were so restrained that for a long time he had not even noticed them; they were what might be expected of an old maid, whose suddenly aroused feelings were mingled with timidity and a long habit of self-respect and obedience to the precepts of her religion. Moreover, she was hampered by the presence of Lise, whom she had never been able to win over, in spite of success with the little boy, who was too young to remember his mother.

A single look at Mélanie was enough to disgust Joachim with Péronne Grenier. Instantly he took in his wife's enduring youth and the charm of her face, which had ensnared him at twenty with the hope that her penniless state might persuade her to become his mistress; he had given in to her charm in spite of himself. Now his look was charged with hate rather than love; this was what made Mélanie shiver. He couldn't help thinking of the vile Séverin, and the joy he must have had from her cheeks and lips and body; but at the same time he banished the heavy-set, hatchet-faced Péronne from his thoughts. The fierceness of his look betrayed a husband who could not bring himself to forgive when the time came for him to call upon Mélanie for an accounting. Yes, this he was resolved to obtain. Yet he had promised Dom Béranger to treat his wife as a servant, and a man doesn't demand an accounting from a servant; he simply accepts her service.

After Péronne had gone, Mélanie wondered if she, in her turn, would be banished. In order to stave off Joachim's all too familiar gesture, she hurried to the stove and proceeded to set the table. She set three places, for she knew she had no right to eat with her husband and children. That didn't matter; she would lay her plate on the drainboard of the sink or stand up and hold it in her hand. Meanwhile she put Pierrot in his seat and tied a napkin around his neck. Lise knew how to take care of herself. But there was a question in the girl's eyes: "Aren't you going to eat with us? . . . I know you're my mother." At that moment, for the first time since their separation, Joachim addressed his wife.

"Is lunch ready?" he asked curtly. "I'm hungry."

Still speechless, she could only nod her head. Lise

had little appetite, and when her father scolded her she burst into tears and was scolded even more gruffly. Mélanie did not dare intervene. She had a feeling that Pierrot was the favorite, and that the little girl, who had never let Péronne Grenier take her mother's place, was cruelly treated— No, Joachim was not really cruel; she was, rather, thrust into second place because of the influence which Péronne had with time acquired over her father. She, Mélanie, would make up for this injustice. But how was she to do so, when she had not even the right to be recognized by her children? Perhaps in a few days recognition would come; she would work with that goal in view. When Joachim went off to his work she would be alone with them; she would have a hand in their upbringing and get them to love her. How thirsty she was for their affection! But her husband was issuing orders:

"This afternoon the children will be off at school; they come home at four o'clock. At half-past four they can have bread and cheese, as much as they want, in spite of the rationing. You're not entitled to any: is that clear? You'll look after the cow and chickens, just like Péronne. And make yourself up a bed in the barn. That's all for now."

And he got up to go back to the sawmill at the lower end of the village, taking Pierrot by the hand, and summoning Lise with a loud oath when she lagged behind with her eyes on her mother.

Mélanie was alone. She had seen her daughter's impulsive gesture, and it had filled her with hope, but only for a moment. Never would she penetrate Joachim's hard heart or win his pardon. Nevertheless, she had humiliated herself; indeed, she would willingly have gone down on her knees if it would have done any good. But Joachim's resentment was a stubborn one. He intended to keep her as a servant, without pay, and to separate her from her children. She was not to sleep in the house; once she had cleared the table and washed the dishes she must go to the barn, a hundred feet behind the house at the end of the vegetable garden, which she would share with the cow. But she had never expected Joachim to readmit her to his bed and board. Her first thought, when her lover had left her, was how to get back to the children. Now she was back, but her torture was greater than ever: she could see them, but they were not to treat her like a mother; she must wait upon them but could not hope to give them a kiss.

In her distress, she thought of running away. But where should she go? To Bovinant, where the old shepherd was lusting for her? She felt nothing but horror for the place where she had lost her soul. To the Grande-Chartreuse monastery, where Dom Béranger would receive her? Yes, but what would he say? She could hear the words he had spoken to her in the confessional of the church of La Ruchère. He had told her to go home, and to win through patience and good conduct her husband's forgiveness and the affection of her son and daughter. The first day was not yet over, and already she had declared herself weary and beaten! . . . How many months of waiting lay ahead!

VI

The Night Brings Counsel

MÉLANIE prepared the children's afternoon tea, of which, Joachim had said, she would have none. Cheese is a commodity just as rare as butter, even in the country. And Mélanie did not mind going without it, quite aside from the prohibition imposed upon her. Pierrot ate his up immediately, but Lise, noticing her mother's abstention, cut her piece in two and offered her half.

"Why aren't you having anything to eat?" she asked.

"Because I'm not hungry."

"You don't have to be hungry for tea. Take some of my cheese."

Mélanie was sorely tempted, for she had stood at the kitchen sink to eat her meager lunch, and now there was an empty feeling in her stomach. Moreover, she was afraid to hurt Lise's tender feelings. And so she forced herself to smile.

"I had some just before you came," she lied.

The little girl accepted this excuse, but went on to ask more boldly:

"Why don't you talk?"

45

Lise understood that there was something mysterious about the presence of this stranger in the place of Péronne Grenier, but she had difficulty in piecing together her memories of five years ago. Instinctively she had known from the start that the stranger was her mother, the mother who was supposedly dead or—worse yet—had been seen wandering like a ghost in the meadows around Bovinant; but on second thought her assurance wavered. Surely her mother would have claimed recognition. To a child such uncertainty is head-splitting, and so now Lise put the question out of her mind and made comparisons favorable to the new servant rather than the old.

"Péronne wasn't nice to me, you know. Every time I disobeyed her she told Father; but when Pierrot was bad she never said a word. I saw right away that you were different."

"But you shouldn't disobey," Mélanie evaded.

"You wouldn't tell on me if I did."

Mélanie smiled complacently. Just then Joachim entered quietly. They had not heard his footsteps on the stair.

"What were you saying?" he asked Lise gruffly.

"Nothing."

"What do you mean, nothing?"

Mélanie stepped in to save the situation.

"She was promising me her—cooperation."

"She has no reason to make you any promises. Get on with your work. And you, Lise, be careful."

And after he had scolded his daughter he announced:

"Tomorrow's Sunday. The curé of Saint-Pierre-d'Entremont is coming to say the eleven o'clock mass here, after the choral mass in his own parish." Turning toward Mélanie, he added: "You're not to go. I forbid it."

She bowed her head, dismayed by a stricture which cut her off from the rest of the population. Every Sunday, from hamlets far and wide, peasants streamed into the village. Although Joachim had told Dom Béranger he would take his wife back as a servant, he had not committed himself to proclaiming the fact in public. It was quite enough for Péronne Grenier to know, and to threaten him with her enmity. Lise was taken aback by her father's intransigence, and when he turned his back to take off his warm jacket she slipped her hand into Mélanie's as a sign of allegiance. But Joachim swung around, noticed the child's gesture and cuffed her ears.

"What kind of behavior is this?"

Mélanie was ready to accept the indignities heaped upon herself; but the manner in which he treated his daughter was hard to bear. From the stove she cast occasional surreptitious glances at him as he bent over to mend the chair which Péronne had broken. He was older, but still as stalwart as a beech. How could she ever have turned to Séverin? She couldn't imagine. Perhaps because of the hardness of her husband's fea-

tures. Séverin was always laughing and making funny
faces.

The evening passed in embarrassed silence, broken
only by a remark from Joachim:

"Children, haven't you anything to say? You're
usually such little chatterboxes."

Pierrot was sleepy, and Lise was enervated. This
end of the day was far from what Mélanie had expected. She had known it would take time to win
Joachim's pardon, but she had thought the children's
hearts would open to her immediately. Instead, she
was not allowed to communicate any feeling to them.
Joachim had instinctively found the way to wound her.
It would be like death to sleep alone in the barn, without hearing their breathing. How many nights she
had awakened at Séverin's side in sudden alarm and,
to his question "What's the matter?" replied only,
"Nothing; just a nightmare." She had kept her anxiety
to herself, knowing that she could not share it. Never
had she confused her maternal feelings with the guilty
love which she had followed not so much of her own
free will as under some strange compulsion. She was
a weak woman, and her husband had pushed her into
temptation with his rough ways instead of succoring
her by some evidence of understanding. In the end we
are responsible for our own fate; but only when it is
too late do we awaken to our responsibility.

After the children had been put to bed Joachim's
silence indicated that it was time for her to retire to

the barn, and she went out, murmuring a good night to which he made no reply. She walked through the vegetable garden to the stall where the cow was chewing her cud. Then she noticed the moon, which cast her shadow near an apple tree. It laid its light like a blue smoke on the side of the mountain, and the rocks of the Chartreuse and the wall of the Granier were as if covered with new snow. She had no desire to sleep, and so after a moment's hesitation she passed beyond the garden hedge and started down the road toward the church. Almost everyone had gone to bed, and the road was deserted. The feeble glow that filtered through the shutters of the tavern was the only sign of life.

Mélanie was surprised to see that the day still maintained its losing struggle with the night. In the paling glimmer the trees were like ghosts around her. The mountain slopes were flooded with an even, color-less light, which stopped at the edge of the forests of beech and pine. Down below, the Frou valley held the Guiers-Vif River, a silvery serpent reflecting the rising moon. Toward the widening horizon wood, water, and rocks mingled in a fairy-tale scene.

Mélanie had been used to watching the sheep on summer nights at Bovinant; and she remembered the distress she had suffered there, thinking of her abandoned children. Now that she had found them again she was even more distressed than before. Now she was the abandoned one: abandoned by a lover who held her in such light esteem that he proposed handing her on to his successor, and by a husband who treated her like a servant rather than the mother of his children. At this point she remembered Dom Béranger's parting words: "You must be patient. I advise you to look to the Virgin of Lourdes and of La Salette. Pray to her whenever you are unhappy, for no one has ever appealed to her in vain."

The façade of the church was as white as snow. In the absence of both priest and sexton, it stood open night and day. No one in the parish was sacrilegious enough to steal the sacred vessels. Mélanie walked down the nave, where the moon was beginning to shine through the stained-glass windows, all the way to the foot of the altar, where she fell on her knees and raised her hands in supplication. But no prayer came to her lips. In the last five years she had not said so much as an "Our Father"; for Séverin had mocked both her scruples and her devotion. Now, so desperate was her need of help that words of prayer finally did come— not those addressed to Our Lord, but the salutation to Our Lady, who is so much closer to us.

No man, and above all no woman, has ever prayed without learning something. As Mélanie expressed sorrow for her sin, she found good counsel. She had left her children for five whole years; surely she could wait a few days or weeks to regain them. Then, before she knew it, the familiar "Hail Mary" came back to her; and as she repeated the rediscovered words she listened attentively, as if Our Lady were about to make a direct reply. Suddenly her feeling of futility and isolation vanished. Were her prayers on the way to fulfillment? In any case, she felt calmed and almost happy, and it was with a confident step that she started toward home.

The moonlight was now as bright as dawn, and the rocky summits of the Chartreuse mountains were one huge patch of snow, blending with the pale sky. From the horizon, muted by the stillness of the night, a medley of musical sounds—the far-away murmur of a mountain stream, the breeze which rustled the leaves of the trees—rose to accompany her on her way. Amid the vast universe she was not alone. Suddenly she heard footsteps on the road behind, and was afraid. Soon the walker overtook her: a man still young whom she recognized. It was Jean Combaz, the wood dealer, who must be on his way back from a business trip to Saint-Pierre-d'Entremont or Les Echelles, heading now for the tavern, which stayed open in defiance of the curfew. In the moonlight, he had recognized her.

"Ah! Mélanie Corbier!" he said mockingly. "It's some time since you've been seen in these parts."

She did not reply, but stopped to let him pass. Instead, he came closer and slipped his hand under her arm.

"Is it all over with the shepherd?" he asked.

She shook off his hand and started to run away, but he caught and held her.

"Not so fast, little lady!"

Mélanie marshaled all her strength and agility. She had told Dom Béranger of slapping Séverin across the face the first time he made advances, and Dom Béranger had indicated approval. Now, as Jean Combaz seized her she wheeled and struck him so hard that he fell to the ground. She ran ahead, slipped through the hedge bordering Joachim's vegetable garden and out of the man's sight. He got up, shook himself, and, because he was just drunk enough to be unsteady, staggered across the road, looking for revenge. Then, failing to find her, he went into the tavern, where a few men still sat around the table.

"Can you guess who I ran into at this late hour?" he asked loudly. "Mélanie Corbier! She wanted me to go with her . . ."

VII

After Church

PÉRONNE GRENIER had already spread the news of Mélanie Corbier's return to La Ruchère, now confirmed by Jean Combaz. And so groups of people stood about the church waiting for the priest to come from Saint-Pierre-d'Entremont and at the same time watching with morbid curiosity for the arrival of Joachim and his children, with Mélanie in their train.

"She has her nerve, that's what I say!"

"Some women are shameless!"

"But Péronne says he treats her like a servant and sends her to sleep in the barn."

"Yes, and, she tried to persuade Jean Combaz to follow her there just last night."

"We'll have to keep an eye on our husbands."

"There's never been a black sheep at La Ruchère."

"Never. If she comes, I'll point my finger at her."

"Ha! Ha! I see Joachim!"

"Where?"

"There, through the trees, coming around the curve in the road."

"The trees are in the way. Is that woman with him?"

"No, I don't see her. Not yet, anyhow."

Just then Joachim Corbier appeared, holding Pierrot by the hand, with Lise a step behind. But there was no sign of Mélanie. The bystanders felt thwarted, for they had expected to make public demonstration of their disapproval. In the usual way the men sat on the right of the nave and the women on the left. No one cared to sit beside a woman who had lived in sin, and the others were prepared to isolate her in case she came in.

There was no reason to show disapproval of Joachim, since he had not displayed her. In the general opinion, he did well to be ashamed. Perhaps he had already sent her back to Bovinant. So much the better. The men, who feared condemnation by the women, nevertheless decided after a moment's hesitation to accept his approach; but no one asked him about Mélanie or commented upon her return. Suddenly the church bell rang three times, summoning all present to come inside, if they wished to obtain a seat rather than stand near the door.

After the mass Joachim was, without realizing it, the object of everyone's attention. There was talk of ration cards, of the price of bread, milk, and eggs, and of means of transportation to Les Echelles and Saint-Pierre-d'Entremont, the last being a subject in which

Joachim was particularly interested. At a certain point Jean Combaz mischievously inquired:

"Have the shepherds come up from Arles to Bovinant?"

A woodman who cut pine trees at the pass answered:

"Yes, some came before, and some after."

By "before," he meant before the influx of a great crowd of refugees from the German invasion of the north of France; by "after," he meant after they had gone back to their native places and the roads were once more unencumbered. (Actually the sheep never traveled on a highway.) No one seemed to catch the reference to Mélanie's seducer. But the men mumbled something about going to the tavern at Reverdy for a drink, since alcohol was not rationed. "Come along," they said to Joachim; "we'll stand you to a glass." That would loosen his tongue and bring out what had become of Mélanie.

Joachim looked around for Lise and Pierrot. Pierrot was in the midst of his school friends, and Lise was in the hands of some old women who professed pity for her motherless state and burned to know the secret of what was going on in her family.

"So Péronne Grenier's taking good care of you and your little brother, is she?"

The child did not guess at their double purpose.

"Péronne left yesterday," she said simply.

"And why did she go?"

"Father sent her away. But he's taken somebody to replace her."

"Oh, really? And who might that be?"

"I don't know."

"Is it anyone you ever saw before?"

"No," she said, blushing.

What made her blush at her own answer? For she blushed as if she were denying her own mother. She blushed like Peter, three times denying his Lord. She blushed because of some obscure unconscious instinct, which opened up like a bubble coming to the surface of the water. The women were on the point of obtaining a description of Péronne's substitute and comparing it to their recollection of Mélanie when the suddenly suspicious Joachim summoned his daughter.

"Lise, come here! You're to take Pierrot home. I'll be with you shortly."

The good women could learn no more. Just as they were about to get something out of Lise, her father had interrupted. And the child, knowing his bad temper, hastened to obey. She found Pierrot playing marbles in a deserted corner of the church square.

"Come, Pierrot," she said, "or else I'll be in for a scolding."

Pierrot paid no attention, and when she seized his arm he burst into tears. Joachim had followed the scene from afar, and now he upbraided his daughter. The injustice of it was almost too much for her to bear. But finally both children started toward home, with the men following behind and stopping off at the Reverdy tavern.

The Turin or Chambery vermouth was not on the ration list, and Jean Combaz, who had made a profitable business deal at Les Echelles, offered a round of drinks to the company.

"Here's luck, everybody! And luck to you, Joachim Corbier! Tomorrow I want you to saw me a dozen cords of wood, which I've contracted to sell. . . . By the way, what's this about your wife? Is she back home?"

Joachim was taken aback by the abruptness of the question and instinctively wriggled out of giving an answer.

"My wife? You must be crazy!"

"I saw her just last night."

"Where?"

"On the road, when I was coming to the tavern."

"That's the first news I've had of her."

Benoît Tornet, the egg merchant, attacked the subject from another angle.

"I hear you've sent away Péronne Grenier."

"Who says so?"

"She does. She told my wife."

"That's right. I didn't need her any more. I've got someone else."

"Your wife, is that it?"

"No, not my wife. A servant to whom I pay no

wages. Once upon a time she may have been my wife, but she isn't any longer."

The listeners were flabbergasted. To convince them, he concluded:

"The best proof is that she's sleeping in the barn."

Jean Combaz was the first to recover from his surprise. On his cheek was still the mark of the blow Mélanie had struck him, and inside him there was considerable liquor that he had drunk to celebrate the sale of his wood.

"Well, I saw her on the road," he said obstinately.

"On the road?"

"Yes, I recognized her in the moonlight, and she spoke to me, besides."

Joachim choked back his anger; but Benoît Tornet would not let the matter go:

"I still say you should have kept Péronne." And he added, in a low voice: "There are some women that have men under their skin."

Joachim heard him perfectly well, but chose to speak to Jean Combaz.

"What did she have to say?" he asked.

Jean Combaz threw out his chest. He was a handsome fellow, and now he laughed as if he had made a conquest.

"Oh, I don't know," he said fatuously. "She said something about being through with her shepherd."

"He's got himself married," Joachim said briefly.

"Oh, so that's why she came running home," said

another man. "Before you took her on as a servant, I hope you gave her a good whipping."

Joachim Corbier rose, leaving his glass half empty. He was visibly irritated now, and no one wanted to provoke him. They all took refuge in collective cowardice.

"It's strictly my own business," he said.

They put on a conciliatory, fawning air.

"Of course, Joachim. You're master in your own house. Finish your drink, and have another."

But he was still vexed and took leave of them with a brusque:

"Goodbye, everybody."

Once he was gone, the men's tongues wagged freely, and the second round of drinks was an absinthe brew. They pinned on him an epithet common even in a village like La Ruchère, where in the memory of the oldest inhabitant there have been no deceived husbands. Up in the mountains, when a girl misbehaves with a boy of her own age their parents see to it that they are married before the baby is born. And that is all the mountain people know of so-called loose morals, for practically never has an unfaithful wife come into their ken. Perhaps the villagers were so hard on Mélanie Corbier because they felt that she was a cause of ignominy and shame to them all. For five years they had forgotten her existence. They had pitied poor Joachim and his abandoned children and praised Péronne Grenier for the effort she had made to take care of them. And now, suddenly, the deserter had come home. She had come because she too had been deserted and had nowhere else to go. No one credited her with a longing for her childen or an earnest desire for forgiveness. No, not one: for her conduct had brought her into low repute, and her husband could not believe in her repentance.

Dom Béranger perhaps had swayed Joachim somewhat when he came with the assurance that she had made her peace with God and deserved to be taken in. Even so, he had received her only as a servant; and the tavern talk left a bad taste in his mouth. What had she been doing in the moonlight on the open road? And what had she actually said to Jean Combaz? As he entered the house, he gave her an ugly glance. She had taken good care of the children, that much was true; they were wearing sandals in place of the dusty shoes in which they had walked home. And while they had been at church she had set the table and prepared a delicious piece of boiled beef, with vegetable cooked in its juice. She had installed Lise and Pierrot on their chairs and tied a napkin around the boy's neck. Now she became aware of Joachim's ill humor and stayed in her corner near the sink, planning to eat after all the others, when they had had enough; but she would not be able to satisfy her hunger, because she could see her husband was on the point of making a scene. Sure enough, as soon as the meal was over, he said to the children: "Run along and play outside."

Before Mélanie could even fill her plate he burst out:

"Why were you out in the moonlight last night, instead of asleep in the barn?"

So Jean Combaz had been talking. But she had nothing to conceal.

"I went to the church."

"To the church? At that late hour?"

"The church was open. Then, when I was coming back Jean Combaz overtook me."

"You went up and spoke to him. What did you say?"

"He was drunk, and I slapped his face."

Joachim was puzzled. If this was true, then Jean Combaz was a liar. When Séverin had been courting her, she had hidden away. Now, probably neither she nor Combaz was telling the truth. In his distress he could make no decision.

"That's not what Jean Combaz says," he mumbled.

"What does he say?" she asked boldly.

Joachim countered with an order instead of a reply.

"You're to sleep in the barn and not on the road. And you'll go no more to church, either by night or by day."

VIII

Lise

THE next day Jean Combaz came with his wagon, drawn by two horses, to the sawmill.

"Here are my beeches, Joachim. I want them cut so that I can haul them to Les Echelles. The turn at the junction of the two roads is a tight one, but still it's wider than the one in the opposite direction, toward Saint-Pierre-d'Entremont."

Joachim Corbier received the logs without a word, but he eyed his visitor keenly. If he had seen the least sign of mockery on his face, he would have reacted with violence. Combaz, too, was watchful; he had not forgotten the scene in the tavern, and he went on trying to cover things up with talk. Joachim remained stubbornly silent. At last he said:

"Very well. I'll do the job. When do you want it?"

"As soon as possible. I'll come around the day after tomorrow."

"No, you'd better wait till the end of the week."

"All right then. You don't seem to be in a mood for talking."

"I have work to do."

They separated without shaking hands. Jean suspected from Joachim's hostility that Mélanie had spoken. And Joachim scrutinized Jean's face for any remaining trace of the blow Mélanie had told of giving him. In any case, the fellow had desired her. Ever since she had been seduced by Séverin, the shepherd from Arles, everyone was after her—that was plain—everyone had the idea that she was an easy prey. And what about himself? He had taken her on as a servant, but with scarcely more than a passing look. To tell the truth, he had not seen much of a change. In the five years since she had left him, or rather since he had banished her to Bovinant and Arles, he had tried to wipe her out of his memory. And with what success? So far, she had not really reentered his mind. Now, as he came back to the house for the noon meal, he stared at her through the open door, looked at her from head to toe. She seemed to be not older but younger, in spite of the signs of weariness on her face. From her tall, shapely body one would have thought she was a girl rather than a woman of thirty, even if she did, at times, have an utterly miserable and forsaken air. Yes, she was capable of changing from one moment to the next. At this point he too was looking at her with the eyes of desire, and he was ashamed of ever having let his thoughts stray to the bony Péronne Grenier.

When he walked in, the table was set. But instead of encouraging Mélanie with thanks or even a nod of the head, he concealed his feelings under a gruff air and once more unjustly attacked Lise for hanging about the new servant and plainly showing her affection.

"That's enough, Lise. Sit here by me, and don't budge."

Lise clung defiantly to her mother and Mélanie, trying to ward off a storm, murmured:

"Lise, do what he tells you."

But Joachim was quicker to react, and gave her a slap.

Lise protested, between sobs: "I didn't do anything wrong."

Instinctively Mélanie made a protective gesture. She wanted to take up the cudgels for Lise, but she was held back by fear of Joachim's anger. Had not Dom Béranger told her to be patient? Tears welled up in her eyes as Joachim said threateningly:

"You two are in league against me."

His ill humor had grown from day to day, and the atmosphere was very nearly unbearable. Péronne Grenier, on the lookout for incidents in the "household," told her friends that soon Joachim would send his wife away and reinstate his neighbor—that is, if she consented to return. Jean Combaz judged from Péronne's gossip that Mélanie was far too insecure to have told tales on him, and when he came for his wood he was quite bold enough to tease Joachim by asking:

"How about your servant? Are you pleased with her?"

"Péronne?"

"No, the new one."

Joachim made answer:

"How about yourself? Aren't you satisfied with the slap she gave you?"

"What slap?"

"The one that sent you to the ground."

Jean Combaz retorted with a volley of filth directed at Mélanie, and the two would have come to blows had not other men arrived at the sawmill just in time to prevent them.

Joachim went home with Jean Combaz' outrageous accusations still buzzing in his ears and chose to torture his wife by picking incessant quarrels not with her but with her daughter. More than once Mélanie was tempted to step in, but she feared to increase his exasperation. After a week during which Lise had ample occasion to note her mother's distress, she returned from school one day and took advantage of Pierrot's going out to play marbles. With a grave air her mother had never seen in her, she voiced a matter which she had already resolved in her own mind.

"I knew."

"What did you know?" asked Mélanie, stroking her cheek.

"That you were my mother."

"Who told you?"

Lise did not answer, but threw her arms around her neck.

"I want to be with you every minute."

"You can't, though. In the daytime it's permissible, but at night—"

"Night's just the same as day."

When Mélanie had washed the dishes and tucked the children into bed she left the house, under her husband's hostile glance, and went up the ladder to the second floor of the barn, over the cow's stall. After making her newly relearned prayers she adjusted the hay-and-straw stuffed mattress. She had scarcely stretched out in her improvised bed when she heard stealthy footsteps in the garden, and she sat bolt upright when the door, whose key had long since been lost, creaked below. She was paralyzed with fear. Was it Jean Combaz, or some other man of the sort, attracted by her bad reputation? Whoever it was, knew the place and was approaching the ladder. Somehow she found the courage to call out:

"Who goes there?"

A low voice, or rather whisper, made reply:

"It's me, Mother!"

A moment later Lise reached the top and threw herself at her mother, exclaiming:

"I've brought my blanket to keep you warm."

"My little Lisette! How did you do it?"

"I waited till Father was asleep, that's all."

"But he may wake up. You'll get a scolding."

"I don't mind. I want to be with you."

"You must be patient—like me."

"It isn't fair." Lise entwined her arms around her mother's neck. "I'm much better off here than in my own bed. The hay's prickly, but I'm with you."

"My darling!"

In the midst of this outpouring of affection, Lise fell asleep. Her mother listened, with unquenchable happiness, to the child's regular breathing; but at the same time she worried over her husband's waking up to find Lise gone. If only he would take it out on his wife, his servant! She would take the blame upon herself and shield Lise from a beating with her own body. It was just what Dom Béranger had imagined: the goat placing herself in the path of the hunter's gun, in order that the kid might have time to run away. Now that Mélanie had made up her mind, she felt happier than at any time since her return. She had won back her daughter, to be her very own, night and day. Now there was Pierrot to be reconquered, and that was another matter. And then—then Joachim, who was the thorniest of all, perhaps impossible. Dom Béranger had given her due warning. It would be a long pull, longer than life itself. Joachim had been abandoned for five years, and he could never forgive her. Never? No, never. His scornful hostility had made that abundantly clear. If only he did not attack her through her child! She would ask that of him, humbly but firmly. She would ask it the very next day when he found Lise and the storm burst.

The storm did not burst the next day but in the night, shortly after midnight. Suddenly the house door opened and shut with a great noise, rousing Mélanie from slumber. Joachim called out in a tremendous, nightmarish voice:

"Lise! Lise!"

Lise woke up with a start and clung fearfully to her mother.

"Don't answer!" she implored.

But Joachim went on calling. He had pulled on his shoes and trousers and was advancing toward the barn. Mélanie escaped from her daughter's embrace and cried out of the window:

"Here she is!"

She was ready to go down the ladder when Joachim called imperiously from below:

"Lise, come down here at once!"

Lise was standing, and said, before her mother could interpose:

"No!"

A crescent moon lit up the scene, of a child martyr offering herself to the executioner. But Mélanie would not let her accept this role. She called her husband by name and went with outstretched arms to meet him at the top of the ladder.

"Punish me for it, Joachim," she said. "Lise is not to blame."

Joachim stopped short. He had been about to give his daughter a sound beating but found himself face to face with his wife, her hair tousled and her nightdress half open. Lise stepped between the two in order to take what was coming to her, but her mother authoritatively pushed her back. Joachim was silent, breathing hard and trying to control himself. His hands hung at his sides, and it was clear that he had given up the idea of the beating; but in order to save face he said angrily:

"Lise, go get in your own bed!"

"No, I won't! I won't go without Mother!"

To the amazement of the women he mastered his rage and said:

"Then get along, the two of you. I'll shut the barn door."

They descended the ladder, and at the bottom they took each other by the hand. Joachim led them through the garden and opened the door of the house. Mélanie followed Lise to the children's room, where Pierrot was sleeping, his fists clenched. She had just started to settle into a broken-down armchair for the rest of the night when her husband came in and pointed to the big bed in the next room.

"This way," he said.

Slowly and incredulously she rose to her feet. Lise said in a low voice:

"No, no! He'll beat you."

"I don't believe he will. Go to sleep. I'll be right

there," said Mélanie, kissing the girl as she tucked her in.

In her husband's eyes she had surprised a lustful look like that given her by the old shepherd even after she had rebuffed him, by Jean Combaz after she had struck him to the ground, and even by Séverin whose music and fine words had seduced her. But she had never imagined that this would be the way of forgiveness.

Joachim Corbier's loud cries had carried far beyond the barn. Péronne Grenier, a light sleeper, had been awakened right away; and opening the shutters of her bedroom window she followed the whole scene. Joachim had run to fetch his daughter from the barn, where she had chosen to go to sleep on the hay with her mother. Then he had brought both wife and daughter back to the house. Yes, his wife! Just think of that! He had chosen to forget her betrayal and the five years she had lived with the wretched Séverin. For so little he had consented to swallow the outrage she had perpetrated upon him, an outrage which extended to the whole village, where faithful wives were the rule.

Péronne did not find it easy to go to sleep again. Even in these last months, when she had felt that Joachim was beginning to take an interest in her, she had not been able to seduce him. And in eight or ten days Mélanie had won him back. Because she must have been the one to take the initiative; that was her specialty. Early in the morning Péronne went from one good housewife to another.

"Do you know what? Joachim has taken back Mélanie."

For one woman who had the sense to say, "Well, she's his wife, after all," nine or ten took it as a personal affront and spoke out against her. And no one mentioned forgiveness.

IX

The Shepherd's Return

THE day after her return to the marriage bed, Mélanie set the usual three places at the table. But Joachim took notice and said gruffly:

"Bring your plate and glass, and sit down."

She obeyed, causing Lise to divide a smile between both parents. As for Pierrot, he showed no surprise: the new servant was eating with them, just like Péronne, and that was all there was to it. Mélanie, emboldened by this new concession, which certified her position as wife and mistress of the house, looked first at her son and then at her husband.

"You can call me Mother," she said.

"Oh, Mother, very good," he said with a burst of laughter.

Yes, the servant had won a speedy promotion!

That evening Pierrot came back from school with a bagful of snails which his innocent school fellows had given him. Innocent boys—but the parents who had put them up to it were not so innocent. He ran to show his mother this collection of mollusks.

"Look, Mother, they have horns."

His mother made him crush them out on the road.

"They're bad for the plants in the garden," she muttered.

Unwillingly, he did what she told him; but when his father came back from the sawmill he complained of the strange woman emptying his bag.

"But I kept one of them, that's especially pretty. He's just coming out of his shell with his horns sticking straight up."

Joachim crushed the snail under his heel and slapped the boy; and the astonished Pierrot held one hand to his reddened cheek, unable to understand why he had been struck, and angry at his father's turning against him instead of Lise. Probably it was because of this woman called Mother who was always sticking up for his sister. He was bitter about it, but Mélanie soothed him with caresses.

The following Sunday, when the curé of Saint-Pierre-d'Entremont was to say mass again, Joachim said to Mélanie in the rough manner in which he continued to address her:

"Get dressed. And in your best clothes, too."

"I've nothing except this one worn gown."

"Well, that can't be helped."

"I'll wear a bright kerchief on my head."

Was it the bright kerchief atop her blond curls that made Mélanie so conspicuous when she walked into the church with her husband and children, Joachim holding himself even more stiffly than usual? No one said a word, but the pews around her remained vacant. She and Lise were left quite alone: although the congregation was large enough to fill the church, the women preferred standing in the back to sitting anywhere near her. The men were more easy-going, or perhaps indifferent. They sat alongside Joachim and Pierrot, but without any sign of recognition. Joachim was so vexed that he did not go to the tavern. He looked at Mélanie even more dourly than before, as if she were responsible for this hostility! She saw now that her misdeeds had exposed her to blame not only by her husband but by the rest of the village. Little had she realized, when she listened to the blandishments of Séverin, that she was dishonoring all the good women of La Ruchère. Surely, now that she had repented her sin, they could be a little more tolerant. Or wasn't tolerance really demanded of them? Yes, it was! Gospel episodes she had heard in her childhood crowded into her mind. Jesus had forgiven Mary Magdalen, and the woman of Samaria. She remembered their stories only vaguely and did not know their full meaning even now that she was a sinner of the same kind. But what about her husband? He had forgiven her only imperfectly, or rather he had not forgiven her at all.

The month of August passed without bringing any change in the household. Although there was no real intimacy, habit gradually made for a regular pattern of daily existence. This was the season for deciding what trees should be chopped down or shorn of their branches, and Joachim was very busy. The children were out of school, and Mélanie had to keep an eye on them, besides mending their clothes for the following winter. She had resumed her machine stitching for the Perrin glove factory at Grenoble, in order to contribute to her husband's income rather than be a drain on it. And the fact that both of them had so much to do all day reduced the strain in their relationship. She knew that her least failure to perform the duties of a wife and mother would bring the house down on her head, and she acquitted herself of those duties not only with love but with punctiliousness.

Was there any likelihood that Joachim's attitude would soften? She went right on hoping. The first half of September had gone by, in the same state of uncertainty, when the thing she most feared came to pass. Séverin, whose marriage had made him an owner as well as a shepherd of sheep, had been seen in the pastures around Bovinant. Perhaps he had come to help the old man take the flock back to the plains. Or was this just a way to cover his wish to pick up his old love affair with Mélanie? In any case, having carefully waited for a moment when Joachim was at the mill and the children were tending the cow in the field some distance away, he came to the house. He did not knock, but surreptitiously opened the door and found Mélanie sitting with her back to him, near the window, mending a pair of Pierrot's drawers. Suddenly two arms were thrown around her and a kiss planted on her face. But just as quickly, she freed herself from the unwelcome embrace and leaped to her feet.

"It's me!" Séverin exclaimed fatuously, as if he were sure of receiving a warm welcome.

But Mélanie was in full possession of her senses.

"Go away!" she shouted.

Séverin only laughed and made as if to kiss her again. She realized at once the danger of being shut up with him, and threw open the door and ran out into the road. Séverin was momentarily stunned, but he soon came to and pursued her. How could a mistress of five years' standing put on such airs when her lover condescended to call? Hot after Séverin ran Péronne Grenier who, ever watchful, had seen him sneak into Joachim's kitchen. But she soon lost the trail, because both pursuer and pursued were younger and spryer than she. Nevertheless, she convinced herself that she knew their secret: Mélanie had surely given way to this clown's advances. Now, as they ran toward the church, a curve in the tree-bordered road hid them from her. The road led also to the sawmill, and it was there that she must carry the bad news.

On the way she heard cries. Were they those of a woman? Then she made out two bodies rolling in the dust, and the woman struggling to her feet and pummeling the man's face with her fists before she resumed her headlong flight. The man managed to get up too; but he was limping, and his face was spattered with blood. Before Péronne could overtake him, he rubbed his leg, let out a volley of oaths, and continued to run after his prey. When Péronne reached the square in front of the church, no one was in sight. She looked and listened, and when she realized that the fugitives were gone, her narrow mind could come to only one conclusion: Joachim must be told! She went on down the road, which passed just in front of the sawmill. In Joachim's capable hands the saw emitted a plaintive, monotonous whistle.

"Joachim, I have news for you!" Péronne shouted.

"Let me alone. I have work to do."

"But it's important."

"Not as important as my work."

She raised her voice above the whir of the saw and shouted into his ear.

"Séverin is here!"

He finished the tree trunk before laying down his job. Then he drew her aside and asked:

"Where did you see him?"

"At your house."

"With—with Mélanie?"

"Mélanie left the house," she admitted. "And he followed after."

"Where did they go?"

"I don't know. I just wanted to tell you."

"Thank you."

With her errand successfully accomplished, Péronne went her way. But Joachim climbed the hill more quickly than she and soon overtook her. He had told his assistant what to do with the timber—for he was meticulous about fulfilling his obligations—and gone off for the express purpose of avenging his honor. On his belt he wore the ax with which he was wont to cut branches. As he reached the church Mélanie came timorously out, looking around her. He roared something at her, and she hurried toward him with outstretched arms.

"Ah, it's you!"

This gesture alone should have him understand that she had held her ground. But jealousy plays havoc with both feeling and reason. Meanwhile Péronne had arrived upon the scene.

"Wait a minute," said Joachim.

He called Péronne and said:

"Did you see Séverin enter my house?"

"Yes, I saw him."

"Oh!" Mélanie cried out in indignation.

"Did you see them leave the house together?"

"Yes, and I saw them roll in the dust of the road."

"Wasn't I scratching his face in self-defense?"

"Yes, but he ran after you."

"I took refuge in the church, and he didn't dare force his will on me there."

Joachim felt that she was telling the truth. But his face was jealously impassive, and he separated the witness from the accused without giving any verdict.

"All right. We'll see. Go on back to the house, while I look for this fellow Séverin. He may be lurking about the barn."

He strode off, leaving the two women together.

"Yes, I saw you, and I saw the shepherd," insisted Péronne.

Mélanie could not find a word of justification. She had an idea that virtuous women do more harm with their slander than the penitent sinners to whom they refuse their pardon. And so she turned her back on her neighbor and walked away, in the same direction as her husband. Was Séverin still hanging about, and would Joachim find him? He was carrying his ax, and that might mean serious trouble. God forbid that blood be shed between them.

But Joachim had found no quarry. No sign of Séverin on the road, in the fields, or anywhere in the vicinity of the house. The children had brought the cow back to the barn. His bad humor persisted. He gave Mélanie no chance to explain, but stuck to the story as he had heard it in front of the church.

After lunch he went to get his rifle out of hiding. By decree in the occupied zone, and even in the unoccupied zone, all arms were to be turned over to the local mayors. Most of the mountain people had guns with which to hunt goats, grouse, and white partridges. When the mayor of La Ruchère had put up the official notice some law-abiding souls turned guns in, but most poachers resolutely hung on to them.

Joachim set out in the direction of Bovinant, with Mélanie calling fearfully after him:

"Where are you going?"

"Hunting," he answered noncommittally.

She understood and she did not move, but stood watching at the door as long as he was in sight. Lise came up to her and asked:

"Is Father going to shoot a goat?"

Then she saw that her mother was crying.

Joachim took the shortest route: around the chimneylike formation of the Petit-Som and the sloping meadows of La Charmine. In the pastures he could see flocks of sheep gathered around their bellwethers. All the flocks from Arles now belonged to Séverin; word to this effect had spread throughout La Ruchère and the neighboring villages. Joachim hid behind a beech tree and watched for the shepherds. But after a whole hour he saw only one, a very old man. He had loaded his rifle with regular cartridges, not the buckshot used for hunting game, and had made no attempt to disguise his purpose. On the way he had met a woodcutter from La Ruchère, who had said: "Hunting's not allowed this year. What's tempting you?" And he had answered: "A two-legged animal." The woodcutter had only nodded, having already heard from Péronne Grenier that Séverin was somewhere around. "Good luck!" was all he had to say. He would never report the crime, and neither would any of his fellows. As long as Mélanie didn't talk, Joachim was sure of going unpunished. Five years before, he had very nearly committed murder, but had thrown his wife out of the house instead. Now that he had taken her back, however ungraciously, he meant to defend her. When he was tired of waiting he hid his gun in some bushes and went to question the old shepherd, who did not know him.

"Where's your master?"

"He went away early this morning and hasn't yet come back," said the old man without suspicion. "He went to see about places to put up for the night on the journey home. Because we're taking our sheep away day after tomorrow by the Col de Porte and Grenoble. Did you want to see him?"

"Yes, there's something I want to talk to him about."

"I can give him the message."

"No, it's not worth while."

And Joachim went back down to La Ruchère. Mélanie had waited all afternoon to hear the echo of a shot among the mountains, but none had sounded. Now she questioned her husband with her eyes, but he said not a word. Was Séverin dead or alive? She had no way of knowing.

X

The Revelation

EVER since he had gone out with his gun after Séverin, Joachim had not merely treated his wife severely; he had submitted her to something like torture. Every evening he plagued her insistently for details of her lover, which she could not or would not relate.

"I've told you everything there is to tell," she murmured humbly.

During one such scene Lise ran from her room in her nightgown to her mother.

"You stay out of it," Joachim shouted.

But the girl, although small and frail, was resolved to take her mother's part. Joachim marched upon her, intending to give her a beating, and Mélanie, like the goat defending her kid, put her own body in the way.

"Don't strike her. Strike me." And she managed to cover the child's flight.

One fine day at the end of September, Joachim returned from the sawmill at noon to find Mélanie missing. The night before, he had handled her roughly, as if she had sunk to the rank of a mere prostitute, selling her body. Even so, she had not reacted, except with tears. Now only three places were set at the table.

"Where's your mother?" he asked.

"She's gone for the day," Lise told him.

"Gone? She should have told me. Where did she go without my permission? Didn't she see fit to inform anyone but you? Where is she?"

"I don't know."

"How long ago did she leave?"

"When Pierrot and I went to school."

"At eight o'clock then, after I had gone to the sawmill. Well, out with it! What did she say to you?"

"She said: 'Lise, it's up to you to get dinner. There's a ham and potatoes. I have to go somewhere.' 'Are you coming back?' 'This evening or tomorrow.' 'Where are you going?' 'Far away.' Then she kissed both of us. I followed her until she disappeared on the path leading into the forest."

"Why didn't you follow her all the way? She must have gone up to the pass."

"Maybe so. Oh, and she said: 'Be good to your father.'"

Joachim was annoyed that his victim should have eluded his grasp, and besides he had a vague consciousness of guilt—although he still felt that a man is master in his own house, especially a man who has burdened himself with a sinner as a servant. He barely touched his lunch and got up from the table saying:

"I'm going to look for her."

As he shut the door he heard Lise murmur:

"Don't be too rough, Father."

What right had she to interfere? He was tempted to answer her severely. Why should he feel sorry? Hadn't he done the right thing? After five years' desertion he had taken his wife back as a servant, for the sake of the children. And then he had reinstalled her in the home. That was unwise, and yet he had done it. Then this fellow Séverin had come back and made advances to her—at least so said Péronne Grenier. She had rebuffed him, or she hadn't: he couldn't really be sure which. It was his right to question and reach his own conclusion—his right as head of the family. The whole parish was on his side. People were ostracizing her to show their disapproval. Could she possibly have gone to Bovinant to look for Séverin? No, all the shepherds had led their sheep back to Arles earlier than usual. He knew, because he had been up to see for himself. Anyhow, if she had left La Ruchère, if she had run away from her prison—yes, her prison!— he would give her the punishment she deserved and bring her home in the proper state of repentance and submission.

As he walked up to the pass, with a gait as regular as that of a guide, only faster—for his heart could stand even the steepest climb—angry thoughts filled his mind. He had been thinking in terms of escape and prison. For wasn't it an escape that she had attempted? Now, naturally enough, he was engaged in pursuit.

Whose fault was it if she was a prisoner? She had surrendered to him voluntarily, when Séverin's marriage had left her all alone. In fact, she had been glad, at that point, to have her former husband take her in. That monk, Dom Béranger, had struck the bargain: he was to take her back as a servant, without wages. He had done this, and then had given her a place in the household. A place? What place? He had given it to her for his own pleasure and satisfaction, without forgiveness in his heart. After Séverin's return he had truly made life hard, even intolerable for her. That was the reason for her flight. Well, from now on he would make it still more intolerable, until she begged for mercy. She was his prisoner, and he would not let her go.

In less than two hours he reached the pass of La Ruchère. While he was catching his breath he let his eyes rove over the familiar landscape, including the peaks of Granier and Corbelet, and the Frou valley where the Guiers-Vif River ran—the tints of mountains, woods, plains and far-off Lake Bourget all blending together in a golden haze. And he thought: If only the fellow has left the Bovinant pastures, as the old shepherd told me! It may still be hot down in Provence at the end of September.

He was about to move on toward the promontory of the Petit-Som and along the path to Bovinant following the contour line, which he felt sure Mélanie had taken, when he saw somebody seated on the stump of a beech tree, where the pass began its descent toward the meadows of La Vacherie and the Grande Chartreuse monastery. Was it a man or a woman, bent over, with chest almost touching the knees? It was a woman. It was Mélanie. He ran down, tapped her shoulder, and said roughly:

"Come along home."

She lifted her pale, exhausted face, streaming with tears and perspiration, but could not utter a single word. Joachim added imperiously:

"If you were looking for your shepherd, he's gone."

"Oh!" she exclaimed in a low voice, expressive of either weariness or indignation.

"Come along quickly. Get up."

She answered, as if she were so short of breath that it was hard to speak:

"I can't."

"How's that? You're a great big, strapping woman."

As he continued to stand over her, she looked up with tears welling out of her eyes, bloodless lips and cheeks as white as the snowy rocks of the Chartreuse mountains. And her silence said eloquently, "Can't you see?"

He was not prepared for this spectacle. Never since her return had he distinguished her from the stones, plants, woods, and water that supply the needs of man. No matter how he had mistreated her, she had reacted no more than an inanimate thing. Indeed, she was his thing, his possession. And yet she was, after all, a thinking, feeling, suffering human being. God grant that she was not ill, ill enough to die! He needed to make her unhappy, and at the same time he was ashamed of his need. He had no real awareness of her personality, but only wanted her to incite his desire and not dare to refuse it. As if she were not anyone's for the asking!

Minutes went by without his realizing his own agitation. Then a miracle took place, and he looked at her with different eyes altogether. Her pale, colorless face shone like that of the girl whom he had made his fiancée after she had, as he well remembered, refused herself to him; it shone all the more brightly in that it was now a woman's face to which sorrow had lent pathos. This face was above desiring; it was like those of the saints in the crude stained-glass windows of country churches, with the Virgin Mary above them and the mass of humanity below. He wished he could take her face in his rough hands and drink of it as one drinks of the fountain of life. But she did not know the working of his mind. She would never comprehend this. Expression is not easy to simple people like them. Still she had an intuitive realization of what was in his mind. The two remained motionless, without speaking.

Obviously she could not yet realize the change which had taken place in her husband. He was still prey to an inward struggle between his man's pride and his repentance. How slowly pride gives way! But his next words were in a very different tone of voice:

"Rest. When you feel better we'll go home together."

She couldn't believe her ears. Joachim still didn't know where she was going. But he no longer supposed that she was going to Séverin. How different was his manner from his usual rough peremptoriness! As she remained silent, he went on:

"The sun's still high over the Grand-Som. We have time to get home before dark. But the September evenings are already short."

She could have gone on and on listening to him.

"I was very hard last night," he continued.

Had he been anything else, since her return? But this unexpected confession touched her to the point of tears. He leaned over and, before sitting down beside her, murmured:

"If you don't mind . . ."

Then she really felt the change. This was not the same Joachim. This was the man who had offered her marriage when she had refused to be his mistress. The five years with Séverin were swept away, and she had returned to the life which she had had with her husband and children before her grave fault.

"Oh, Joachim!" was all that she could say.

He sat down beside her on the stump and took her into his arms, even if somewhat timidly. There she once more burst into tears. Leaning against his shoulder, she managed to say what she had sworn to say on the first day of her return—what he had cut off by treating her like a servant:

"Do you for—"

He broke in. "Me—me, too—"

"Oh, no!"

She admitted he, in the rigor of his righteousness, had inflicted torments upon her. Now that the enmity between them had fallen he asked:

"Were you trying to escape from your prison?"

She shook her head.

"Then where were you going?"

"Down there?"

"To the monastery?"

"Yes, to see Father Béranger."

"And what did you want with him?"

"To ask him for the courage to—"

"The courage?"

"The courage to face death."

"Death?"

She managed to smile.

"I haven't long to live. Just look at me carefully."

He looked at her searchingly, looked past the soft skin which had attracted his kisses, to her inner body. Although his feeling had completely changed, and he had been touched as if by a miracle, it was without a suspicion that death shone through her transparent features. Now he guessed at it and protested:

"You can't die now."

"Now?"

"Now that we're really together again. I'll go see Father Béranger. We'll go together."

"I can't make it. Climbing to the pass, I thought I was going to choke."

"I'll help you to get back home. I'm strong enough to carry you, if need be."

"If you'll just let me hold your arm, I can make it."

They got up from the stump, and Joachim put his arm around her waist to support her. A half-hour later a faintness came over her. He picked her up, and she threw her arms around his neck in order to lighten his burden.

"You're not so heavy, you know," he said, forcing a smile.

Nevertheless, at the foot of the slope, he was staggering, and she insisted upon walking again. Night was falling when they came to the house. Péronne Grenier at her window saw them. She would have news to spread the following day: "She seemed to be drunk. She went in the morning to find her shepherd. Her husband brought her back in the evening. Either she was drunk, or he had given her a beating."

Lise was waiting at the door. She was surprised to see her father holding her mother in his arms. She ran to Mélanie, and Joachim told her, almost smiling in spite of his fatigue and anxiety:

"You can see I haven't been so rough with her . . ."

XI

The Trip to Les Echelles

OCTOBER and November passed, and bad weather came to the Chartreuse country: wind that howled through the pine trees as if over a storm-tossed sea, rain that changed quickly into snow. Why did the parish no longer see Mélanie Corbier at the Sunday mass celebrated by the curé of Saint-Pierre-d'Entremont (although it hoped now soon to have its own curé)? The women, the virtuous women (for all the women were virtuous at La Ruchère) decided to ostracize her and her daughter completely, for Péronne Grenier told them that she had gone in search of her shepherd at Bovinant and that her husband had brought her back, so drunk that she could not walk, that is, unless he had beaten her up, as he had every right to do. But their plan did not work, because their victim did not show her face. Joachim must have shut her up in the house. Not such a bad idea, at that; you can't be too careful when you're dealing with a female.

Joachim seemed to be taciturn and harassed when he came to church with the children. That was understandable, for Mélanie was not the most restful of companions. People were sorry for him, but they didn't inquire about his wife. Joachim was proud, and he was not sociable; he worked hard at the sawmill, and people went to him on business, not for conversation. Lise and Pierrot, on the other hand, were gay and full of laughter. They were clean and neatly dressed and were a credit to their father. For their mother, no one had a good word to say.

Péronne, ever vigilant at her window, had this to report about the relations between husband and wife: "She goes into the garden to pick vegetables and flowers. She picks chrysanthemums, the kind with which we deck the cemetery on All Souls' Day. At dusk, when Joachim comes home, he insists upon her going into the house. He won't let her stick her nose outside in this bad weather, and yet she's big and strong. He must be afraid she'll slip away under cover of darkness. He's holding her prisoner, and I can't say that I blame him."

Little did Péronne know what happiness and sorrow dwelt in Joachim's home together. Early in December, when the roads were already obstructed by snow, Joachim hired a mule and drove his carryall to Les Echelles, which together with Entre-Deux-Guiers, is a sizable town on the border between Savoie and Isère. Here the Guiers-Mort from the Chartreuse mountains, and the Guiers-Vif, from the Frou valley, flow together.

"He's gone to get an order from a wood merchant," explained Péronne, who had witnessed his departure.

Instead, Joachim had gone to fetch the doctor. At La Ruchère people did not call a doctor except in serious and desperate cases. But Péronne was ready with an explanation. She had seen Mélanie at the door and noticed that she was pale and unhealthy. Doubtless she had an ailing stomach, perhaps a cancer sent by God in punishment of her sins. Péronne had seen Joachim gathering mushrooms, and so there was also a chance that he had poisoned his wife with a toadstool, then felt sorry and gone for the doctor. In any case, he brought the doctor up and took him back in the carryall that same afternoon, with chains on the wheels to prevent them from slipping in the newly fallen snow.

Several local people met the travelers on the way and stared at them. Péronne's explanation allayed their curiosity. Toadstools are notoriously dangerous. But surely Joachim wasn't a murderer. Wasn't he, though? On that score, the woodcutter who had met him when he was pursuing Séverin with his gun, had a story to tell.

Joachim had had difficulty in persuading his wife to let the doctor come. She insisted that she wasn't really ill, or at least that she would soon be better. It was expensive to bring the doctor all the way from Les Echelles, just because she couldn't go down there for a consultation; and it seemed unlikely that he would find any definite symptom. But, after several weeks, she was persuaded.

Dr. Villard examined this woman whose body had once been so muscular, supple, and well proportioned; and he found it no more than a skeleton. The lungs were intact, but the heart was beating slowly and at increasingly long intervals. Now and then heart and pulse stopped entirely, as if they might not beat again. Fortunately, warned by her husband, the doctor had brought a syringe and some camphor solution. He made some injections straightway and taught Joachim, who was clever with his hands, how to manipulate the needle. When they were out of Mélanie's hearing he said:

"It's only a matter of days."

"Days!" Joachim exclaimed in horror.

The doctor thought well to soften the effect:

"Or weeks, perhaps; or even months."

Joachim seemed to be on the point of collapse.

"But . . ." he began.

"But what? Please finish your sentence."

"But we've just made up after a long quarrel."

The doctor may have been surprised, but he took it calmly.

"My prescription will cover almost anything that can happen. But you'll have to watch her night and day. She may even get well. Before this heart trouble came upon her she was a healthy woman. How can she have contracted it?"

Joachim took the blame:

"I'll tell you: it's my fault."

The doctor smiled incredulously. As if heart disease could have any other than a physical cause, as if it could be brought on by mere sorrow! Before climbing into the carriage he said:

"It's snowing. Winter's early this year. I don't enjoy coming up to La Ruchère in bad weather. Be sure to do what I told you. You have medicine. Give her one or two injections a day, depending on how she seems. And here's luck to you! There's always the chance of a miracle, when the cure's beyond our power. . . . You've put chains on the wheels, I see. That is wise."

The two men said very little on the way down. At the doctor's house in Les Echelles, Joachim paid the contracted fee and turned back in the darkness. Alone with his thoughts, tears ran down his cheeks. But as he drew near La Ruchère he became increasingly hopeful: There's always the chance of a miracle. Why not? And he was able to face his wife serenely. The next morning he called his daughter aside.

"Can I depend on you?" he asked.

Lise smiled. "What for?"

"For your mother."

"Yes, absolutely."

"Then you're not to go to school. Pierrot will go alone and tell the teacher you're ill. I have to earn money at the sawmill, and so you must look after your mother during the day. There are pills and potions she must take from hour to hour. Only you must make no mistake about them. It's all written down in the doctor's prescription. You're a reliable girl, I know. Now, you must play the part of a nurse."

Lise became serious. The trust placed in her was great, involving a grave responsibility.

"I'll make no mistake, Father—you can be sure of that."

"Then you're day nurse. That's official."

"And what about the night?"

"At night I'll be on duty myself."

"I'm strong, Father. I can take care of her both day and night. You need to sleep."

"No, no. After all, you're a young girl, less than twelve years old."

"I'll be twelve very soon."

She started to question him about matters beyond her understanding. She didn't know how much to say, because the idea of death was incomprehensible to her.

"Is Mother very ill? She isn't ill enough to—to die, is she?"

"Don't say that! Be quiet! We're going to save her."

"Yes," she echoed with assurance. "I'll save her with those medicines."

Joachim thought of something else.

"You'd better keep Pierrot at home with you. If she has a fit of choking, he can run to fetch me. We can't count on our next-door neighbor."

"You mean Péronne? She's a bad woman."

Lise had guessed it. She knew that there were enemies all around them.

"If she starts choking, you must help her into a sitting position and prop her up on pillows. Can you do that?"

"Yes, I can."

In the next room the invalid was surprised by this secret consultation. She forced a smile.

"What are you two plotting against me? I might even get up. The doctor said I could."

"No. He said only for two or three hours in the afternoon."

"And what about my housework?"

"Lise will do that."

"Lise? She's too little."

Lise made a laughing protest.

"I'm quite big enough, thank you!"

The month of December was going by, and Mélanie was getting steadily worse. Joachim repeated to himself the phrase of Dr. Villard: "There's always the chance of a miracle." At dawn of the day before Christmas, he scrutinized the weather and found that, after a week of fog and snow, there were prospects of a clear, sunny day. He could easily get over the pass of La Ruchère and down to the monastery on the snow-shoes which he had kept from his days in the army. Skis might seem faster, but they would be cumbersome both going up and coming down, where the pine trees were too close together. Moreover, they would inter-fere with his plan. After he had sniffed the air, he came back into the room where his wife lay, propped up on several pillows.

"I'm going away for the day, little one," he said. (For some weeks now, he had addressed her in this manner, as if she could count on him completely.) "Don't worry."

"Don't go!" she begged him.

"I'm going to the Grande Chartreuse, to see Father Béranger."

She caught her breath and managed to say:

"Because I'm—going to die?"

"No, to help you live."

"Will you bring him back with you?"

"Yes, I promise."

"Dress warmly, and take care of yourself," she said in a strangled voice.

A miracle, that was it, a miracle. Only a man of God could bring it to them. Dom Béranger had brought Mélanie back to the home where he had so cruelly received her. Now the man of God must fulfill his mission by bringing her back to life. Ever since he had set his heart upon this plan, Joachim was hopeful. Once more he gave instructions to Lise.

"The medicine is all in order. It's your job to look after her while I'm away."

And he set out, joyfully, taking long steps on his showshoes, toward the pass of La Ruchère.

XII

Joachim's Pilgrimage

S IX months had gone by since the return of the
Carthusian monks to their monastery. The
Grande Chartreuse, high amid the snows, had partly
reinstated its cloistered life and rule; but most of the
cells were not yet rebuilt and the damage caused to
walls and interiors by years of abandonment was not
so much repaired as covered over. From the vast empty
expanse of mountains and forests, the monks' prayers
rose into the sky like coils of smoke over village roof-
tops, indicating the presence of human life below.
After thirty-seven years of absence, this Christmas
was to be celebrated with particular fervor, and now,
on the eve of the feast, the sun shone with unusual
brightness on the monastery and was dazzlingly reflected by the rocky heights of the Grand-Som.

In the months since the armistice few visitors had
traveled so far. But now, at ten or eleven o'clock in
the morning, one stood at the gate. His worn coat was
festooned with bits of frost that had fallen from the
trees, a woolen cap covered his head and ears, and his
snowshoes were heavy with snow. He wore heavy

gloves and held a pick in one hand. The lay brother at the gate took pity and invited him in to warm himself and drink a glass of the famous green chartreuse, which has the power to restore a man's body.

"Where have you come from, that you are so cold?"

"From the other side of the mountain. It wasn't easy to get over the pass, with two or three feet of snow. Luckily I had my snowshoes."

"And what do you want here?"

"To see one of the monks."

"You know that our rule obliges them to close confinement. Are you looking for anyone in particular?"

"Yes, for Father Béranger. He knows me."

"Tell me your name."

"Joachim Corbier, from La Ruchère. Perhaps he's more likely to remember my wife. I must speak to him."

"The Fathers can't be seen at this hour."

"Very well, I'll wait. But I must take him back with me before sunset."

"Take him back where?"

"To La Ruchère, of course."

The lay brother could not help laughing.

"Dom Béranger? But he's sixty years old! Besides, he's not supposed to leave the monastery."

Joachim made a peremptory gesture.

"I'm sure he'll come. Just let him know, as soon as you can, that I'm here."

"I'll ask the Prior to give Dom Béranger permission to see you."

To the brother's surprise, the Prior conferred with Dom Béranger and then gave him permission to receive his guest in the parlor.

The monk walked straight to the visitor. "I remember you, Joachim. Did you come over the pass without skis?"

"I had my snowshoes . . ."

Dom Béranger had not forgotten the family tragedy, but he had never learned its outcome. Had husband and wife been reconciled? Had the servant returned to her wifely status? Had the man's pride allowed him to forgive her? His visitor was too intimidated to know what to say or even where to begin his story.

"You've come alone, Joachim Corbier. This is no weather for bringing your wife. Please give me news of her."

"Father, she's dying."

"Dying? She was young and seemed perfectly strong. What could strike her down so suddenly?"

"I've killed her, Father."

"Miserable fellow! You struck her?"

"No, nothing like that. I've shortened her life by tormenting her."

"Tormenting her?"

"Yes, over her shepherd."

"You weren't able to forgive?"

"No, Father, I wasn't."

"She came back to you repentant. You should have asked God to soften your heart."

"I thought about it more than once, but let the days go by; and then it was too late."

"How did it come about, Joachim? And what brings you here when the pass is blocked with snow?"

"A miracle is necessary. You alone can do it. I can't."

"A miracle? God alone can perform a miracle, directly or through His saints."

"There's got to be a miracle. She must be cured—for my children and their happiness."

"Look not to me, my son, but to God. But tell me your story."

"Well, Father, I'll begin with the day in July you came to me. When I returned home for lunch the table was set and a hot meal was waiting. She had cleaned the house, and it looked better than it had for a long time. I had to admit that. And the children were neat and clean. They stared at her, but she didn't dare speak to them. I walked right in front of her as if she weren't there. She had even placed Pierrot on his chair with a napkin around his neck to protect his clothes. Then she waited on us at the table, and herself stood in a corner to eat. In the evening she did the same and then went to bed in the barn. This went on for eight days. On the ninth evening, Lise disappeared while I was sleeping. I called for her everywhere. Finally I went to the barn and found her with her hair full of straw. 'Where were you? Why are you not in your bed?' 'I don't want my bed any longer.' 'You're being very silly. Go back to bed.' 'I want to sleep with Mother.' She was so resolute that even a beating wouldn't have made her obey. I let her have her way. I was a coward."

"You were kind."

"Perhaps it comes to the same thing."

"You're wrong, Joachim. Cowardice is a weakness of the flesh. Kindness is an impulse of the heart."

Joachim suspended his narration, as if it were very hard to continue. Dom Béranger had to urge him on.

"That same night I took my wife in. Oh, it wasn't for the children's sake; it was for my own."

"You did well, Joachim. She is your legitimate wife, your wife before God and men, and your wife purified by the sacrament of penance."

"Yes, if I had taken her back in that spirit. Anyhow, after that we lived together. The children were happy, and were beautifully cared for. They had a good time with her. But she laughed only when she was with them."

"Why not with you, Joachim?"

"Because I was still cruel."

"Didn't you love her, my son?"

104

"It was because I did love her—because I was jealous."

"Explain yourself. I don't understand, or else I understand too well."

"I wanted her for myself alone."

"But she had already become wholly yours."

"I wanted to possess her entire past. That fellow Séverin came back one day. She ran away from him and hid in the church. A malicious woman told me my wife had listened to him; and I listened to the woman. It wasn't true. Then I questioned Mélanie about him. The more I desired her, the more I tormented her with questions. She only cried or said nothing. In this misery she offered to go away, all alone. But I held her—I kept her chained, you might say. She was my prisoner. I didn't notice that she was wasting away. One day when I came back at noon from the sawmill I couldn't find her. I asked my daughter: 'Where's she gone?' She told me that her mother had gone for the day, that she had taken the path to the pass. I said to myself: She's gone to be with her shepherd. It was the end of September, when the sheep go back to the plain: but they had gone already. Without knowing this, I went looking for Séverin to kill him."

"Kill him?"

"Yes, I meant to shoot him."

"God punishes us for taking vengeance into our own hands. And your wife had put that guilty love behind her."

"He had left Bovinant. But she didn't know it."

"You were sure that that was where she had gone?"

"No, Father. It was out of my jealousy that I accused her. Stopping at the top of the pass to catch my breath, I saw my wife resting on a stump beside the path to the Grande Chartreuse. I said brutally: 'Are you going after your shepherd?' She looked up at me with such horror that I couldn't doubt her any longer. All at once I understood, and I began to burn inside. I realized that she was going to you, to enlist your aid against the torment and imprisonment to which I had subjected her, and that she couldn't walk a single step farther, because she was at death's door. I took her into my arms and begged her forgiveness. She cried, but she said it was for joy. Ever since that day I've been at peace with myself. It was as if a heavy weight had been lifted from me. The whole house was different. We were very close to one another, man, woman, and children. And then at the beginning of December she had to take to her bed. Before that she had forced herself to go on—because Christmas was coming, and the children's Christmas tree. And now, Father, she's going to die."

"I'm sorry for you, Joachim, with all my heart."

"I'm much more of a sinner than she. I had her, and now I have lost her, all through my own fault. If I had opened wide my door and my heart to her, she would be well today. I treated her first like a servant and then like a loose woman. And now I'm a very unhappy man."

"What about the children, Joachim?"

"The children? I think Lise understands. She's nearly twelve years old, and mature for her age. She adores her mother, and perhaps she will hate me for what I have done."

Dom Béranger reflected on all that his visitor, who was now silent, had told him.

"Yes, Joachim," he said at last. "You have sinned more than she. She was the body, and you were the spirit. You had an opportunity to give her peace and happiness and the family life to which she was so eager to return, and you let it escape you. Not often do we have the opportunity to show ourselves at our best. Return home, and be kinder to your wife in death than you have been in life. You tell me it is only a matter of days. The pass at La Ruchère is open: you have just come over it. Have something to eat, and then start before evening."

Dom Béranger rose to go for the lay brother in charge of the refectory. But Joachim timidly stretched out a hand to detain him. He still had a few words to say.

"Wait, Father. I want to ask you a great favor."

"If the rule allows me, I'll do it."

"The doctor that I brought from Les Echelles

told me after examining my wife: 'It would take a miracle to save her.' And you can perform that miracle."

"I?" said Dom Béranger sharply.

"You, and you alone. She trusts you so completely! For three days I've been thinking about it. I thought about it all the way through the snow. I beg of you, Father, yes, on my knees—"

As he was about to kneel, Dom Béranger stopped him.

"No, you mustn't kneel, except before God, the Virgin, and the saints!"

"You brought her home; but it's not enough to bring her home to die. You must make her live. I'm discharging upon you the sin I committed in tormenting her. I'm discharging all my sins upon you, and you must plead with God for a miracle."

"You must pray to God yourself."

"I'm a poor man, in trouble. I don't know what to do. I haven't even been able to tell my wife how much I care for her. Up here in the mountains we don't know how to talk."

"But you did ask her forgiveness, after your repentance."

"Yes, as well as I knew how."

"Then you can only pray, my son. I'll be praying too. On this Christmas Eve I shall pray for you especially."

Joachim felt in these words a sympathetic but

none the less firm refusal, and exclaimed in despair:

"But, Father, we're completely alone! At La Ruchère everyone is hostile to us. Not a single man or woman will hold out a hand; in fact, the whole parish is waiting eagerly to see what kind of trouble we'll get into next. People treat Mélanie like a leper, and she's dying all alone, with only Lise to attend her. No blessing, no sacrament. It seems as if even God—"

"No, Joachim, you mustn't doubt God. Is there still no curé at La Ruchère?"

When Joachim shook his head Dom Béranger stepped impulsively toward him.

"Very well, then; I'll go, if I can obtain the Prior's permission. I'll go this very evening."

"Oh, you'll perform the miracle!"

"The miracle is in God's hands. But I can at least bring comfort to her last hours."

"Father, I expect more from you than that. I'm hoping you'll bring her back to life."

"Resurrection? Eternal life, perhaps. I'll take the holy oil to her."

"When do we leave, Father?"

"I'll go to the Prior. Wait here for me."

It was with fiery eloquence that Dom Béranger told the Prior Joachim's story, down to the desertion of the Corbier family by the whole parish. The Prior was touched.

"Yes, the lost sheep. There is more joy to the shepherd in its return than in the safety of all the rest of the flock together. Go along to La Ruchère. But the pass is obstructed by snow. How will you get there?"

"The brother who buys our supplies has a pair of snowshoes. He will lend them to me."

"Do you know how to use them?"

"I was in the Chasseurs Alpins. So I am accustomed to both snowshoes and skis."

"But you're sixty years old. Are you sure the trip won't be too much for you. You'll carry the holy oil."

"God will sustain me. And I shall have as companion Joachim Corbier, a sturdy woodcutter."

"Then God go with you!"

Dom Béranger returned to the parlor.

"I have the Prior's permission," he said. "We'll have a bite to eat and then be off while the weather is still fair."

Before leaving he tucked inside his jacket the holy oil and the consecrated Host. Joachim eyed him appraisingly.

"Father, in spite of your age and your white beard, I believe you're a strong man."

"My beard turned white before its time," Dom Béranger answered, "but my heart and legs are good."

After Notre-Dame de Casalibus, when the climb became steep, they had the footprints Joachim had made to guide them among the frost-laden trees. At the top of the pass a broad view into the distance spread before their eyes: the peaks of the Granier and the

Cobelet framing the Frou valley and, far away, Lake Bourget. The landscape was a uniform white with the speck of water an emerald-green. The white rocks rivaled the snow under a sky of a magnificent blue seen only in winter, a triumphant blue which joined with the sun to lift up the whole earth. In spite of the shortness of the December day, the travelers reached the village before dusk.

Dom Béranger, under his companion's watchful eye, had managed the ascent well although his breathing became somewhat labored. At the summit he paused, as much to enjoy the beauties of creation as to catch his breath; and he cried:

"God be praised!"

Joachim took this cry as the promise of a miracle.

XIII

Christmas Eve

HAPPY-GO-LUCKY Pierrot took advantage of this sunny day to put on the little skis made for him by his father. Indefatigable, he climbed up by the Grand-Crêt, the Grand-Bassin and the Grand-Village and then slid proudly down, trying hard to keep his balance in spite of the gathering speed. He fell two or three times but got up like a little man, without crying. Toward evening he saw his father, accompanied by a man in a white cassock. Instead of bounding to meet them he preceded them to the house, calling out:

"Lise, Lise! Here's Father, with an old priest."

Lise relayed the news to her mother, who received it with a mixture of nervousness and joy. So her husband had succeeded. He had brought Dom Béranger back. This was the beginning of the miracle. She propped herself up on a pile of pillows and, breathing hard, managed to slip on the woolen sweater Lise brought her.

The living quarters of the Corbiers, at the top of a flight of stone steps which separated them from the damp ground, consisted of an ample kitchen, where they ate their meals; on the right a big bedroom with a fireplace where, for Mélanie's sake, a wood fire blazed night and day, and the children's room; on the left, across a hall, an unused room where a stove had been placed for the monk, in case he came. Mélanie questioned Lise with her eyes, for talking fatigued her. And Lise understood. In recent weeks she had learned the meaning of her mother's every expression.

"Yes, Mother, I made the bed in the spare room, in case he wants to rest there. There's hot water in the kitchen, and brandy and sugar for a grog, if he and Father want a drink when they arrive. There's a clean cloth on the table. I hear them now!"

At the bottom of the stairs the men scraped their snowshoes and took them off. Joachim led the way up the steps and into the house. Dom Béranger was close to exhaustion. Crossing over the pass had taken four to five hours and, at his age, had been a heavy tax on his heart and legs. Joachim offered him the only armchair in the kitchen, which was drawn up before the fire, and Lise came forward with a hot drink.

"No, no," said Dom Béranger, straightening up his weary body. "First of all, I wish to see the sick woman."

"Oh, you're very kind!" said Joachim. He opened the bedroom door and announced joyfully: "Mélanie! Mélanie! Here's a visitor for you!"

She was waiting tensely. In Dom Béranger, mind had quickly reasserted its dominion and he was again master of himself. Now suddenly he remembered the woman who had come to the monastery six months before, her cheeks glowing with health, a handsome, blonde woman whose features he had almost immediately forgotten, in imitation of St. Francis of Sales, who says that we must lose individual faces in the love of God. Here before him was a pale, bloodless, dry-lipped, panting creature, with death written on her face, except in her dilated, dark eyes, which glowed with supernatural light. Suddenly he felt as if he had gone back to the time more than twenty years before, when he had returned from the other war to find his wife and daughter stricken with the influenza which was soon to carry them away. He relived momentarily those hours of despair, which had somehow restored his faith in God. Now, by the sublimation of his own human affections, he was called upon to impose acceptance of the supreme sacrifice upon this woman and this man. And their acceptance would be the miracle for which they implored.

"Madame," he said, "your husband has brought me to La Ruchère. It is contrary to the rule of our Order, but he was so persuasive that the Prior allowed me to come."

Mélanie's eyes were veiled with tears, and she spoke in a hesitant, toneless voice.

"Thank you, Father."

Dom Béranger had promised to put into words

feelings which Joachim found so very hard to express.

"Yes, your husband has spoken to me about you, telling the whole story. He bitterly repents having given you such a shabby welcome and subjected you to so much torment. He loved you too much, or rather, since there's no such thing as too much love, he loved you badly. Because to love means to give rather than to receive, to share God's beneficent love for his creation. Now he has attained this kind of love. He told me that ever since the day when he found you sitting on a stump, on your way to the monastery, he has known happiness and peace. The house was transformed, and the family—man, wife and children—became as one. True happiness is there. It was there all along."

Mélanie stretched her gaunt arms toward her husband. From a stranger's lips she had learned what she had hoped and suspected, but could not know except from Joachim's awkward silence and caresses. She was filled to overflowing with the joy of love, but at the same time remorse for her sin was reawakened. How could she have lived with the shepherd five long years? Why had Joachim let her go? If only she had lain in front of the door, and he had walked over her, then, at least, she would never have gone to Bovinant. After these troubled thoughts she turned to Dom Béranger and repeated in a low voice the last words he had spoken, which she took to refer to her death.

"Happiness was there all along." And she added: "Father, will you hear my confession?"

Dom Béranger sent away Joachim and the children, even Lise, who was pursuing him with a drink of hot grog.

"Later, little girl, later. I have business with a soul."

"But it's hot, Father," the child insisted, and Mélanie added:

"Yes, drink it!"

Dom Béranger did, and gained added strength for his task. When he was left alone with the dying woman he pulled a chair over beside her bed, in order to spare her all possible fatigue, and spoke first, by way of encouragement.

"Here I am, my very dear daughter. Your husband tells me that you have been patient and gentle: patient before his scorn and anger, gentle as a lamb before his hardheartedness. And more than once you defended your daughter from his threats."

For the second time Dom Béranger remembered the goat that had protected the kid with her own body. On the way over the pass, the woodcutter had told him of the family quarrels, taking the blame for them upon himself and tardily exonerating his wife.

But Mélanie wept to hear her husband's praise, and made feeble gestures of denial. Finally, though it was hard to talk, she said:

"Father, I am afraid to die in so much sin."

"My daughter, you confessed yourself in the church, before I went to call on your husband. When I brought you back to him, you had made your peace with God."

"That's not enough. It was for my own sake that I wanted to come home. I lived in sin five whole years. For my husband, for my children, for me, nothing can wipe out the shame and horror of that."

Before this despair born of mistrust of her own powers of expiation, the monk pointed out that Christ had carried her sins, along with His cross, to Calvary, and given Himself in propitiation. Drawing upon the colloquy of St. Angela of Foligno with the Savior, he brought before her eyes the sufferings which Christ offered up for our offenses:

"Christ speaks to you through my voice, my daughter. Listen to what He has to say: For the sins of thy shoulders, my shoulders have borne the cross; for the sins of thy hands and arms, my hands were pierced by heavy nails and hammered to the cross, so that my arms had to bear the full weight of my body. For the sins of thy heart, which succumbed to erring desires, my heart was run through by a spear, and from this wound blood and water ran out in order to redeem thee from anger and sorrow. For the sins of thy feet, which carried thee to places of perdition and drew thee into indecent dances, nails were driven through my feet, and the blood running out of them joined the blood streaming from my body. For all the sins of thy body, for the sensuality of thy days and nights, I was struck as I hung upon the cross. I was bathed from head to foot in blood and sweat, and the wood of the cross burned and pressed upon my body. Amid this mortal pain I cried out for help and I died groaning. . . . Thus Christ speaks to you, through my unworthy voice, my daughter. Thus He reassures you. You must be comforted and die serenely, holding out your arms toward the Virgin, toward Christ, toward God."

Mélanie folded her hands on her breast and murmured:

"This is the miracle."

"What did you say, my daughter?"

"This is the miracle. Now it's not difficult to die."

"I am going to raise my hand and pronounce the absolution."

She received it with devout fervor, and smiled:

"Now Christ has taken upon Himself the burden of my sins. It's a heavy load . . ."

The priest answered:

"I'm going to call your husband and children, so that they may be present at your communion and at the extreme unction."

"Oh, did you bring the Host?"

And so the family was gathered together. Dom Béranger took little Pierrot, now quiet and solemn, as an acolyte and asked Lise to prepare a table for the rolls of cotton and the holy oil. Then he anointed Mélanie's forehead, lips, hands, heart, and feet and made the sign of the cross over them. Her face was in complete repose, happy, as if the last sacrament had eased her body by ridding her limbs and lips and heart of everything impure. Joachim knelt at his wife's side, clasping her hand, which was so thin that the wedding ring slipped off her finger.

"Take it," she said to him in a low voice. "I don't need it any longer—the miracle is here."

"Oh, you're feeling better," he said, rising to his feet with a sudden hope.

"The miracle!" she repeated.

"I knew that the Father would heal you."

"Yes, he has healed me—but not the way you think."

XIV

The Lost Sheep

DOM BÉRANGER, Joachim, and Pierrot had gone back to the kitchen. Lise stayed with her mother, but when Mélanie became aware of her presence she found words with which to send her away.

"I'm quite all right—I need rest. You had best look after their supper. They must be hungry."

While Lise was setting the table, Dom Béranger said:

"In a few hours Christmas will be here. And there is still no priest at La Ruchère. Are there any plans for a midnight mass?"

"No, Father."

"What if I were to say one?"

"I'm afraid nobody would be there."

"And what if I were to announce it?"

"Someone would have to ring the bell. That means finding the sexton."

"And what about sending the neighbors to find him?"

"The only neighbor is Péronne Grenier."

"Who is Péronne Grenier?"

"Ask Lise."

And Lise spoke right up:

"She's a bad woman."

"Yes," said Joachim, "she's worse than the child can know. It's thanks to her that the whole parish hates us."

Dom Béranger reflected upon this hate, of which he had already learned from his conversation with Joachim at the monastery and along the way. And he came to the conclusion that the good people of the village had been misled by appearances and did not realize how presumptuous and hypocritical they were to sit in judgment upon a supposed sinner. When he had finished supper he rose from the table and said:

"I'm going over to the neighbor."

"To Péronne?" Joachim exclaimed in surprise.

"Yes, to tell her what a mistake she has made and to have her instruct the sexton to ring the bell as loud as he can to announce the midnight mass."

"You'll find her door barred."

"Then she'll have to withdraw the bars."

The children were gaping. They thought of their neighbor as an enemy who was constantly spying upon them. Now, with their father, they went to the window, not to peer through the shutters but to hear what took place. The monk climbed the steps and knocked discreetly at the door. There was no reply. He knocked louder and louder, he drummed with his fingers. His voice could be heard. A moment later he went in.

Péronne Grenier bowed respectfully before Dom Béranger's white habit. He in turn did not hesitate, but went directly to the point, with a gravity and a majesty which was enhanced by his tall figure and his white beard:

"Madame or Mademoiselle, I have come to tell you that you have been grossly unfair to your neighbors, the Corbiers. Mélanie Corbier is a good woman, who has made amends for her sin; and, having won God's forgiveness, she has won that of her husband as well. Now she is dying. In order to repair the damage you have done to her good name, you must tell her virtue abroad before she is dead. Is that clear? In three or four hours, I shall officiate in the church of La Ruchère. You seem to be strong and healthy: I ask you to put on a warm coat—it's a cold night—find the sexton and instruct him to ring the bell, and then knock at one door after another to announce the mass and at the same time correct the misinformation you have spread about the Corbiers."

To this speech, uttered with authority, Péronne could not find any answer.

"You understand," the monk insisted. "First, tell the sexton to ring the bell; next, spread the truth about Mélanie Corbier. You misunderstood the situation; that is the only excuse you can offer."

Péronne Grenier's conscience was not easy; but

her attitude of ill will toward her neighbors was deeply ingrained. Grumblingly she protested:

"I never said a thing."

"You spread slander about her, but God, in His goodness, has given you time to make amends for your error. The time is short, because Mélanie Corbier has only a few days to live. I have just given her extreme unction, and this sacrament often has the effect of prolonging life or at least of making death more peaceful."

"Oh, did you come all the way from the Grande Chartreuse to be with her, Father?"

"Yes, the Prior gave me special permission."

"She repented at the last moment."

"No, she repented six months ago, when she came back to her husband. But you refused to believe that she was sincere. Everyone at La Ruchère looked on her with suspicion, and perhaps that is your fault. She deserved a warm welcome, and instead, on your account, everyone turned away from her. You must make up for it, and without delay."

The monk spoke with such conviction that he won over even this enemy, who consciously or unconsciously was aware of her wrongdoing. Where most of humanity is concerned, ill will prevails over good, but there are times when the latter triumphantly appeals to reason. Still, Péronne was not exactly tenderhearted, and she persisted in her stubbornness.

"Very well, Father, since you are here to guarantee the story. Nobody's going to believe me, you know.

But if you make a pronouncement, everybody will be brought around."

By her refusal to spread the truth, Dom Béranger was able to measure the extent of the hostility which had poisoned the Corbiers' lives. And because, in spite of the monastic life, he was still a man of action, he promptly decided what to do.

"I'll speak, then. I'll have my say at the midnight mass. Meanwhile there's no time to be lost."

"Oh, so you'll speak!"

"Quickly now. Tell the sexton to ring the bell."

"Yes, Father, I'll be off at once, in spite of the cold. He'll need help to make ready the church."

"I'm counting on you, Péronne Grenier."

Proud of the mission with which she had been entrusted, she went out with Dom Béranger, who returned to the Corbiers'. Mélanie was resting peacefully, with her husband at her side. The children had gone to bed: Pierrot, worn out by his attempts to ski, was already sleeping; but Lise lay on top of the covers, fully dressed, with her ears keen for the slightest sound. Dom Béranger, after looking in on Mélanie, retired to the room which had been prepared for him and settled down by the stove to write the sermon he had promised to deliver at the midnight mass. At nine o'clock the church bell rang out in the clear dry air which had followed the snow. He listened to it: Péronne Grenier had persuaded the sexton. And now, in every one of the hamlets which made up La Ruchère, houses were suddenly lighted. The mountain people had understood the meaning of the bell, rung every half-hour so that no one should fail to hear it.

Toward eleven o'clock, Joachim knocked at the priest's door. His face was pale and sad, but he was perfectly contained, as he accepted God's will.

"It's all over, Father," he said.

The monk rose and put his arms around him:

"On the contrary, my son, this is just the beginning. Believe me. I too had a wife and lost her. I understand your sorrow. Mine brought me to God."

"She woke up and tossed about. She could feel my hand holding hers. I'm not sure she saw me. She said: 'You, and Lise, and Pierrot . . .' Then I thought she'd go back to sleep, but she had difficulty in breathing. After that, in spite of the hoarseness of her voice, I distinctly heard her say: 'This is the miracle—it's life . . .' She choked for a moment, and then relaxed and lay still, as if she were asleep, asleep forever. I knew that she had gone without suffering, for she didn't make another sound. Come, Father."

Lise was already in her mother's room.

"She's dead, then," she said dully, ignorant of the full meaning of the word but guessing at its significance; and her child's body was shaken with sobs.

Dom Béranger took her too into his arms: "No, she lives. Her last words were: 'This is the miracle—it's life . . .' She's gone to heaven, little Lise, and from there she'll watch over you all, especially you, since you'll be your father's companion. God took my wife and my daughter both from me, but you, Joachim, are fortunate enough to keep your little girl. No, don't wake Pierrot. He'll learn the news tomorrow morning. I am going to say for her and for you the prayer for the dying."

He knelt at the foot of the bed, and Joachim and Lise followed his example. "Depart from this world, Christian soul . . .

"And now, while you watch over her, I must go to the church."

"It's cold. Take this cape," said Joachim, who seemed to have already inherited some of the thoughtfulness of his wife. "And be careful not to slip on the icy road."

"I'm used to that."

Dom Béranger went down the road from Reverdy toward the church. He overtook people coming from the hamlets higher up: Grand-Crêt, Grand-Bassin and Grand-Village."

"So you're going to say a midnight mass for us, Father?" they said.

"Yes, I've just given extreme unction to the wife of Joachim Corbier."

"Is she so very ill?"

"She died just a few minutes ago. She was a good woman."

"Are you sure of that?"

"Absolutely sure. And you were wrong, you and your wives, to give her such a cold welcome."

Dom Béranger lost no time in his effort to change public opinion. Thus, too, he was preparing his listeners for his sermon. The whole parish was present, including many children, who would be glad in future years to remember this midnight mass held in a year of war and enemy occupation. The monk slipped over his white cassock the alb and chasuble appropriate to the occasion. The church was so crowded that the warmth of the people's bodies drove back the cold air from outside, and their collective breath formed first a halo and then a cloud around the burning candles. Dom Béranger read the gospel story of a Savior come to earth in the shape of a babe in a manger, with an ox and an ass to adore him. Then, to the surprise of the congregation, he took off his vestments and mounted the pulpit. He began by recalling the angel's appearance to the shepherds; and, having traveled in the Holy Land, he was able to describe the flocks of sheep which still gather around Solomon's wells, in the vicinity of Bethlehem. The shepherds had come first, before the Magi, before the great in the world, to bring their offering to the Infant Jesus. Jesus, grown to be a man, acknowledged their homage by comparing Himself to them. "I am the good shepherd," he told his disciples; "and I know, and am known of mine. As the Father knoweth me, and I know the Father:

and I lay down my life for the sheep." From these verses he passed easily to those others: "What man of you that hath an hundred sheep: and if he shall lose one of them, doth he not go after that which was lost, until he find it? And when he hath found it, lay it upon his shoulders, rejoicing: and coming home, call together his friends and neighbors, saying to them: Rejoice with me, because I have found my sheep that was lost?"

For a minute or two Dom Béranger remained silent, in order to let the meaning of the parable become clear. Then he proceeded to draw a parallel with the story of Mélanie, which was familiar to everyone present:

"Well, my brothers, the shepherd did not have to go far to find this lost sheep, for she came back to the fold alone and of her own free will. Alone she trod the rough road, with thorns and brambles on either side. The shepherd should have been quick to rejoice, but he was slow in seeing. And as for the rest of you, good people of La Ruchère, you did not rejoice at all over the lost sheep's return; on the contrary, you were hostile, hypocritically hostile to her. Not a single one of you took pity on this humble woman, whose home-coming and death were marked by divinely inspired resignation. Charity covers a multitude of sins. But when charity is absent, then there is all too much room for pride and self-satisfaction. Surely I need say no more, on this Christmas Eve, in order to awaken your brotherly love. I can be sure that, before this mass proceeds to the consecration and communion, all of you will make amends in your hearts to this good woman and those of her family who survive her. May the Infant Jesus welcome you as He welcomed the shepherds, and give you His blessing."

The news of Mélanie Corbier's death had already been made known to all the congregation, and now the reference to the lost sheep brought tears of repentance. After the mass was over, Péronne Grenier publicly accused herself of having stirred up and increased the parish's animosity. Jean Combaz admitted to having suffered a rebuff, accompanied by a blow which sent him to the ground. Some of the villagers, both men and women, had demonstrated their ill will to Pierrot by filling his school bag with snails—but not to Lise, in whose presence they did not dare slander her mother. No one was guiltless of hostile behavior to one member or another of the Corbier family, above all to the rejected and ostracized Mélanie. This unbroken ill feeling was just what the monk had condemned and vanquished with his sermon.

Now, as the people went back to their hamlets, through the bright night in which the stars seemed to be closer than usual to the mountains of Savoy, they sought an equally unanimous way of demonstrating their compassion, and not only their compassion but also their friendship for Joachim and his children, survivors of the woman whom they had so grievously wronged. Who knows what man or woman was responsible for the choice of their homage?

For on Christmas Day the whole male population of La Ruchère went to cut the top branches of the pine trees (whose loss does not stunt their growth), to shake them free of snow and scatter them over the road from the Corbiers' home at Reverdy all the way to the church and the adjacent cemetery. Over the route followed by the funeral procession, with Dom Béranger at its head, the mayor and three aldermen bearing the coffin and the mothers of the four largest families carrying the cords in their hands, the evergreens were like palm leaves, symbols of love and praise to God and of rejoicing for the lost sheep whom He had taken home.